What's A Sista To Do

Yvette Way

ISBN: 979-8-9883662-1-8

Acknowledgements

First I would like to thank God. I hear people saying thanking God is cliché. It could never be cliché. I secondly like to thank my mother; may she continue to rest easy. It is her strength and work ethic that has been my inspiration. To the rest of my family and friends. I love you infinitely. I don't I don't say it enough but I hope you know. I want to also thank the people who are always pushing me to write, even when I went through it creatively.

CHAPTER 1

It's New Year's Eve and you know what that means... Parties. Men. Liquor. If you're lucky you'll get all three. At least that's the scenario of most of the New Year's Eves in my adult years. My girls and I get dressed up, find a party or several parties, and find men.

Every year we say it's going to be different and that we are going to be lucky enough to find the "One." Me, I have never been lucky. I don't have a good track record when it comes to dating. I usually meet Mr. Wrong or someone that becomes Mr. Wrong, really quick. Just the thought of some of the men in my past makes me cringe!

This year is going to be different. I can feel it. I have done a lot of soul searching and self-improvement and I am going to find Mr. Right and we are going to be right. There will be no drama and things will work out for my girls and me. So, what's a sista to do? Put on the flyest dress in her closet, some heels, and get her hair and nails did something fierce and prepare for a new year and a new beginning.

If you can't tell by my enthusiasm I don't really like New Year's Eve. On New Year's Eve all I usually get is drama, more drama, and then other people's drama. But once again I feel that this year is going to be different so I am looking forward to this New Year's Eve and the New Year.

Our plan for the night is to go to the New Year's Eve Platinum Ball at Dynasty Ballroom in Saugus. This is the second year the event is being held and if last year is any indication, this year is going to be off the chain. Last year the place was packed, the music was good, and the men were out in full force. I know word of mouth is the best advertisement and there were enough mouths to get the word out.

I looked myself up and down in the mirror. I had to say damn! I've definitely outdone myself. My hair is up in a roll with strands properly placed around my head and my make up is flawless. I managed to find the perfect color red lipstick and foundation to match my cocoa-colored skin perfectly.

The dress I am wearing is red and halter style. It is cut low enough to tease in the front and low enough to let the hounds breathe down my back in the back. Then there is the slit in the front that goes up my left leg. I had to work out intensely for three months to look right in this dress. I'm a thick girl but it is finally in all the right places.

Red is a good color for my cocoa complexion. Growing up my mother told me to stay away from wearing red but now it definitely does the job for a sista. I was watching myself in the mirror, remembering how my mother wouldn't buy me red clothes or any other bright color, no matter how much I wanted them. She would say someone with your complexion should stick to neutral colors. Needless to say I had a lot of black and brown in my wardrobe.

The limo arrived outside my house before I was ready to go. I am rushing around with one shoe on, looking for the other shoe and my earrings. I could hear Imani and Destiny yelling at the top their lungs for me to hurry up. It is already 10:30 and they wanted to be there by midnight to toast and ring in the year.

When I came out the cheers and jeers began. Imani and Destiny got out the limo to hug me. After we greeted and checked out what each one of us is wearing we were all set to get back into the limo.

"Look at this trick!" Imani said.

Destiny just looked me up and down, saying, "OOOHHHH!!"

Imani was wearing a dark hunter green satin gown with a corset type top and long fitted skirt bottom. The dress totally showed off her figure and her complexion. Imani is the true definition of a "trophy-type" woman, her complexion is golden yellow, not high yellow. She has long brownish hair that is streaked with blond, a small waist, round breast, and ass.

Destiny is wearing a little black dress complete with spaghetti straps and a slit up the back. Destiny is also a thick girl but in a more conventional way. Most of her weight is in her thighs and butt. She is only 5'4", which made the long gown accentuate her thighs.

The first thing I did when I got in the limo was smack Imani in the head for calling me a trick. Imani rolled her eyes at me and said, "You know better than to touch a black woman's head, especially when her hair looks this good. Do you know how long I had to sit in the salon to get it looking like this?"

I asked Imani why she didn't go with Jaloni to his away game so they could be together to ring in the New Year. Imani's answer was the same as it usually was when we asked about Jaloni, "Jaloni is acting "Shitty."" She continued, "He was acting like he didn't want me to go. I am single and free for New Year's Eve and looking for trouble."

Imani got quiet for a while like she is contemplating what she said. She shook her head up and down before she began talking again.

"He is probably doing his thing so why shouldn't I do my thing?" Imani asked while rolling her eyes.

On that note everyone left it alone and toasted to "Trouble" with the complimentary champagne in the limo.

I began thinking that it is definitely going to be a drama filled night. It usually is when Imani is not getting along with Jaloni. The drama is not always of the negative persuasion but there is always drama. Imani sees herself replacing Jaloni or keeping the score even but she never leaves Jaloni. I don't actually think she will ever leave Jaloni.

The traffic was crazy all over the city but especially when we reached the ballroom. This is the main reason we decided to get the limo. The fact that the limo was a metallic charcoal color stretch Hummer on chrome is a plus. If you must floss, floss to the fullest is our motto and we are definitely living it tonight.

When the limo got us close as it could to the door the driver let us know he couldn't go any further because he'd never get back out. We stepped out of the limo into the mayhem. We checked each other out once again. We smoothed each other's clothes, fixed each other's hair, and checked each other's makeup.

After that was complete each of us did our final catwalk struts and spins for approval. There had to be approval because we would not let each other look anything less than perfect. Upon the determination that we were all looking fierce we headed toward the VIP entrance, totally anticipating whatever the night had in store.

Men and women were checking us out. Even women with their men were staring at us as they pulled their men closer to them. I personally never understood it. I have been told it is an insecurity thing. When an attached woman sees a woman or women who are alone she feels that they are after a man, any man, including her man. She has to look to size up the competition. I feel if your man is not looking, don't look. Your looking is like

4

giving him an invitation to look. Of course he wants to see what you are looking at.

One guy did look when his girlfriend looked and even waved "hi." His girlfriend immediately smacked him in the head. We couldn't help laughing at them. She started walking in our direction when we began to laugh but her boyfriend had the good sense to pull her back. She was yelling something at the top of her lungs. We just kept walking and laughing because we knew that she really knew better than to approach three sistas.

We wouldn't have been bothered with her anyway. Women like that love to get in fights with women that look better than them in hopes of messing up their hair or clothes. Also, that's not our style or why we are here and the guy wasn't even worth fighting over.

I first saw him when I turned around to go in the door. He is about 6'5" with a Godiva chocolate complexion, dimples, and a head full of black curls. He had a full-length mink coat on which made me think he was a partygoer. I couldn't tell what else he had on but the package itself looked so good and was finished off with chocolate-colored gators.

I found out he was one of the bouncers when we got to the door. As a rule I don't date people that work at clubs because there are too many opportunities for them to fool around. Every night being around girls with almost no clothes on, that would do anything just to get in the club free, something is bound to happen. I'm not insecure in the least bit but I am not stupid either.

There are exceptions to every rule though. I will definitely be looking for that later on, if only for some fun. Yeah definitely! He is just too fine to pass up. I can't stop staring so I know I will have to find him later on. I hope he will be coming inside.

Chingy's, Right Therre, was playing when we walked in the VIP room. Some guys on the wall began pointing and saying Right Therre as we passed. One of them even had the nerve to whistle at us like he on a construction site. It took all of our energy to keep Imani from walking over smacking them all. She hated that kind of immature behavior and had no tolerance for it. Imani rolled her eyes to alert them to her disapproval as we continued pulling her in the opposite direction.

They were not the type of men Imani would talk to anyway. She likes her men proper. You know the type who is all about making money and willing to spend their money on a woman. She likes these men because they can and will wine and dine her. Her favorite saying is "Why not, dammit? I'm worth it."

On the flip side Imani would get with a thug in a minute if he approached her right. It's a weakness or at least that is what Imani calls it. "If he is a smooth looking thug type, I can definitely see him." Imani would say. She likes them strong, dark, and hard core. Imani's a beautiful woman and knows she can turn any man's head. She definitely uses it to her advantage.

That was how she met Jaloni. He was awed from the moment she walked into the charity event he and his teammates were throwing. Imani decided to work this event because she knew it was being thrown by the Celtics. She figured some players from the Celtics and the Patriots would be there.

Imani's boss kept hounding her to do charity work and was very impressed when she signed up for the event. The fact that her boss was impressed was a definite plus. It was one of the biggest charity events of the year and her boss was constantly reminding people to sign up. Needless to say Imani left the event with Jaloni and a promotion.

Jaloni began asking around about Imani from the moment she came in the door. He was ready to pay someone for any information that may have. None of Jaloni's teammates knew Imani. That made Jaloni very happy. To him that meant that Imani is not a groupie. Imani's boss was one of the people Jaloni asked for information. She took one look at Jaloni and decided he is good enough for Imani and brought him over for an introduction.

Jaloni watched Imani periodically throughout the event. He wanted to see if she gravitated toward any of the well-known athletes that were at the function. She didn't, as a matter of fact she didn't really talk to anyone other than the people she worked with and the people she was serving. Jaloni was so impressed by her class and style. He was glad that her boss introduced them and he told himself that he is going to strike up a conversation with her when he finished his assigned tasks.

They talked for a long time after the event. Jaloni thought about asking her out for a cup of coffee or dinner but didn't want to come off as a pushy or arrogant athlete. Imani forgot that she came in the van with her co-workers so she thought nothing of it when they left about a half-hour ago. Imani really didn't have any other way of getting back to her car so she accepted Jaloni's offer for a ride.

Jaloni gave Imani a ride to her car after they went out for coffee. They talked until Imani announced that she had to get up early to go to work in the morning so she had to leave. Jaloni was upset the night had to end but didn't push it. He wanted to make sure that she was who he thought she was so there was no rush on his part.

He asked Imani for her phone number as he walked her to her car. She didn't give it to him but asked him for his. To her surprise, Jaloni gave it to her without the hesitation that men sometime have. Imani was extremely impressed by this. She was also impressed at the fact that they talked to each other for so long and none of the talk was sexual or the "ooh you're so fine" talk. At that time Imani wasn't sure who Jaloni was because she did not watch sports but she did know that she liked him.

She inquired about Jaloni to some of her male friends as well as her father. After they told her who he is, she called him and they set up a date. Jaloni told Imani straight out that he was surprised she called. He thought she wasn't interested because she didn't give him her number.

To make a long story short, they went out and have been together for over a year now. It hasn't been perfect but what relationship is? According to Imani, they have both had their indiscretions during that time but they love each other. This is the answer she has for all of their problems. They love each other.

After calming Imani, down we decided to walk through the VIP room into other ballrooms. There were three ballrooms and it took longer than we thought it would. Every few minutes one of us was being stopped and asked for our vitals (Name? Age? What you doing out alone looking like that on New Year's Eve? Where's your man?). You know the usual tired opening lines. It took so long that the next thing we heard was that it is almost time for the New Year's countdown. We made a run for the VIP room so we could toast with the "good champagne."

In our dash, we waved brothas off and laughed at the fact we were running in our heels over champagne. I lost my shoe and tripped but Imani and Destiny kept running. I tried to play it off but when I turned to take another step, I bumped right into the bouncer from the front door.

He took off the fur coat and is looking too good. I mean the body is big and tight! He is wearing a chocolate-colored sweater and suede pants. He is just chocolate all over. Very nice I thought. Very nice!

He asked if I was OK. I looked up at his face. He looked so sincere and wasn't laughing. I said, "Yes." and looked around for Imani and Destiny. "I can't believe they left me," is all I could manage to say, quickly changing the subject from my fall.

I know I am staring at him. I also know I just tripped in front of him and I am embarrassed about both of these things. Luckily he broke the silence by saying, "I'm sorry your friends left you but you know what they say, if you start the New Year off with a fine man, you'll spend the whole year with a fine man."

"A fine man huh? Aren't you full of yourself?" I responded sarcastically.

I was trying to play it off because this man is definitely fine.

He said, "No, not at all."

He winked his eye and smiled a broad smile that showed off his dimples. I began thinking, "Damn! Dimples too? Is there anything this man does not have?" I was thinking so hard I hoped I didn't say it out loud. I don't think I did because he didn't respond.

He waved a waitress over and ordered a bottle of Cristal and told her to get it here before the New Year. He introduced himself, telling me his name is Darrell. I told him my name is Denise and he repeated them together, ""Darrell and Denise." I like that. I like that a lot."

He began questioning me about what I do for a living, for fun, etc. This shocked me because usually it's the female that shoots off back-to-back questions like that. Coming out of my shock, I answered with a smile, "Aren't you nosy?"

He laughed, gave me a surprise look, and said, "Ouch. I don't need to know that badly. I just figured I better ask you quick or I won't have the chance."

He was still laughing and smiling and I was still staring.

At that moment the waitress returned with the champagne. He tipped her $50 and looked over at me to see if I was impressed. I wasn't. I was thinking he is showing off and knows he is going to miss that $50 and the cost of the champagne next week. Those thoughts didn't stop me from accepting a glass when he offered. What? You can't ring in the New Year without champagne.

Countdown! Ten, Nine, Eight, Seven, Six, Five, Four, Three, Two, One! Happy New Year! Everyone is shouting Happy New Year and kissing. I turned to him to say Happy New Year and he kissed me. I mean he kissed me like we have been married for years and knew each other inside out. The kiss made me tingle inside and out. I was so shocked I didn't know what else to say, "I bet my girls are looking for me. I'll see you later."

He answered, "You bet you will."

I blushed and ran off, hoping I didn't trip again.

I ran right into Destiny and Imani and their questions when I got back to the VIP ballroom.

"Where were you? How could you not toast the New Year with us?" Destiny asked.

"Who is he, heifer?" Imani demanded to know.

I said that he was nobody but I couldn't get Darrell or that kiss off my mind.

CHAPTER 2

We spent the rest of the night looking for what we came for, "Trouble". There didn't seem to be any "Trouble" or any men that were as impressive as Darrell. I wanted to go look for him but I didn't want to seem desperate or easy. That's no way to start things off. It's probably for the best anyway because New Year's Eve flings don't last and I'm not looking for a man anyway.

The men were wall-to-wall but they were also holding the wall up. There were only a couple of people on the dance floor, mostly couples enjoying a night out together. You could tell that because of the chemistry they shared. Seeing this made me a little envious but I like I said, I am not looking.

A group of men stopped Imani. One asked her how she got so beautiful. He continued by telling her it's a shame that she got all those looks when there are so many women that could have used some of her beauty. He then told her that she could have shared her beauty and still been fine.

She giggled like a schoolgirl. He had Imani right where he wanted her. They quickly became immersed in conversation. His boys took that to mean that her girls are now there for the taking. One of them approached me and the other approached Destiny.

The guy that approached me was cute, young, and looked it. He asked me for my name and I asked him for his age and ID. I don't talk to younger men so I didn't care if he thought I was being rude. He took offense to what I said and began cursing at me. I left it alone and smiled because he reminded me why I didn't date younger men.

Imani took one look at him after he started cursing and said. "If you can't take a joke, bounce and go change your diaper because you are sounding real stank right now."

His boys laughed but he just stood their getting even more

heated. He began cursing at Imani until he realized that Imani wasn't backing down. He then lost it and lunged at Imani, raising his hand up like he was about to slap her.

Imani saw this and was ready to fight back, dress, high heels, and all. She backed up momentarily to take her heels off. Just as she jumped back in the kid's face Darrell and about four other men came over to break it up. They pulled this idiot out of Imani's face.

"What is going on here?" Darrell asked looking at everyone like we were all guilty of something.

"He must be crazy, raising his hand at me like I'm his mama or something. I will bust his ass." Imani answered pointing her finger at the guy.

Darrell looked at Imani in amazement. He couldn't believe that someone so beautiful was talking like that. Then he looked at me momentarily. When he snapped back to reality, he and the other men escorted the guy out of the club. I could hear Darrell telling him it is not cool to jump in a woman's face like she is one of his homeboys.

After escorting the guy out the door they came back to ask if we were OK. They also told the guy that originally tried to talk to Imani that baby face said for him to come on or he was going to leave him. The guy nodded at them to let them know he understood. He then moved back over to continue his conversation with Imani.

Imani quickly said laughing, "You had Baby Huey drive you here?"

He answered slyly, "Yeah someone had to be the designated driver, my Benz is at home."

He smiled like Imani was supposed to be impressed.

Imani told him to go home and get it and meet her back here in an hour. She told him she would be out front waiting. She had a devious smile on her face when she said it then looked him up and down seductively. Just as she did, one of the bouncers recognized Imani and asked out loud if she is Jaloni Johnson's girlfriend.

This messed up her game completely. She hated that part of being a basketball player's girlfriend. Everyone knows your name and your business. She smiled an annoyed smile at the man and nodded yes. Homeboy threw his hands up and said, "I can't compete with that. Nice meeting you beautiful."

While he walked off, he mumbled something about all women being alike and gold diggers.

After he left, Darrell approached me with a big grin on his face and said.

"You didn't have to stage this big commotion to see me again. You could have just looked for me or asked someone. Everyone knows me."

My answer was, "I bet they do especially the females." He looked at me and said, "A few of them but none of them could get me. It takes a special woman to get me."

Darrell came close to my face and winked.

I shook my head and said, "So full of yourself."

We both laughed.

He said, "On a more serious note, am I going to get your number this time or next time I see you."

I said, "Next time?"

Darrell said, "Oh yeah! There will be next times until I get your number."

All the guys that came with him to break up the commotion were leaving. As they left they said "Later Boss" to Darrell and went their separate ways. He nodded to them and turned back to me.

"Well lady? What's it going to be?" He reached in his pocket and pulled out a pen, like he knew that I was going to give him my number. He even wrote my name for me, all the while singing Darrell and Denise like he was earlier.

I gave him the number and told him that I only gave it to him to shut him up. He said, "I'll take a sympathy number from a beautiful woman."

He walked off smiling, saying he was going to call the minute he got home. I smiled as I watched him walk away and hoped he didn't notice me watching.

My good mood was interrupted by Imani's comment after he left. She said, "Eww! Why are you talking to the help?" She was laughing but I was not amused. I told Imani to go to hell and turned around to say something to Destiny but she was gone.

"Where's Destiny?" I asked Imani.

Imani started again, "It's so hard to keep track of you hoes. If I was a pimp, I would be broke."

There was nothing I could say to that so I just stared at Imani. She saw me staring and asked, "What?"

We began walking around looking for Destiny. We took time out of our search to continue enjoying the night. After searching for Destiny for about an hour, we gave up and decided Destiny is nowhere to be found. We know her cell phone is in the limo because we all left our cell phones in the limo. Imani and I decided we are calling it a night.

We dragged ourselves to the limo. We were so tired that we weren't laughing or talking anymore. On the way home our minds wandered, thinking we should go back and continue to look for Destiny. It isn't like her to just disappear. She is the calm one in the group. She isn't man crazy like Imani and me.

"Where could she have gone?" I asked Imani. "Did you see when she walked off? Did we check the bathroom?"

Imani laughed at me. "She probably just found one of her ex-boyfriends or something and left with him. She still should have told us before leaving. I'm going to cuss her out when I see her."

We were still discussing the possibilities when the limo stopped at my house. I hugged Imani and told her good night. I picked up Destiny's cell phone as I got out the limo. I was still worrying about Destiny as I dragged myself in the house. I waved back at Imani and the limo as I went inside my door.

All in all, it was a calm night, I thought as I began to get ready for bed. The drama was minor with the exception of a near brawl and Destiny's disappearance. I was laughing just thinking about the things that happened. I was also thinking that it wasn't a bad New Year's Eve at all.

Then I began to think about Darrell. Damn he is fine! I kept picturing our kiss in my mind as I began to drift off to sleep. I was almost asleep when the phone rang. I picked up the phone and yelled, "Destiny is that you?"

The person on the other said yes but it was a man's voice. I was about to ask what he did with Destiny when the person continued,

"How nice of you to realize that so early in the game, that way there will be no confusion." He then said, "No ser this is Darrell."

He then asked, "Who is Destiny?"

"My friend who was with me last night," I answered.

He confusingly said, "I thought her name is Imani because a few people that know her told me her name."

I told him, "Destiny is my other friend."

He said, "I only saw two of you when everything settled down."

I thought to myself that means Destiny disappeared sometime before or during the commotion. Now I am really worried.

He asked, "Did you call her house?"

I told him, "I did but there is no answer. I have her cell phone."

He answered, "I hate to say it but then there is nothing you can do until tomorrow. She'll either show up or you can call the police."

I told him, "I know but it just isn't like her to disappear and not say anything."

At that moment, it hit me that I was talking to him at 4:30 in the morning.

"Why are you calling me this late?" I asked.

He said, "I told you I was going to call you as soon as I got home. This also lets you know that there is no woman in my bed. I know you were wondering."

"Cut the cocky act, it is not cute or amusing. I'm not thinking about you. Didn't you just hear me say that my friend is missing?" I said before I knew what I was saying.

He said, "I am just being me but we can start over in the morning or when you are feeling better. Good night beautiful and I hope you find your friend."

CHAPTER 3

The phone rang at 3 o'clock the next afternoon. I turned over to answer it, hoping it was Darrell so I could apologize for being so harsh to him. I really didn't mean to say those things to him and I wasn't upset that he called. He was sort of getting on my nerves though. I laughed it off and answered the phone.

This time it was Destiny and she is asking me to pick her up. I asked her where she is and she tells me she is not really sure.

I asked her, "What happened to you?"

Destiny's answered, "I'm not really sure and I don't want to talk about it right now."

"OK. Well ask someone where you are." I said to her, still wondering if she is OK.

She came back on the phone and said, "Brockton."

Destiny then put the person that she asked on the phone to give me directions.

I could have lost my mind.

When Destiny got back on the phone I asked her, "How did you get all the way down there from Saugus and not know it?"

She began crying so I left it alone. I told her to give me a ½ hour. She said OK and hung up the phone.

After I hung up from talking to Destiny my mind began to wander. It is really not like Destiny to just disappear and it is especially not like her to go somewhere she did not know. I tried to flip through my memory to see if any of her exes lived in Brockton but couldn't think of any. I just hope she is there of her own free will because the crying is really scaring me. Destiny is not a person that cries a lot as a matter of fact I don't think I ever remember her crying.

Destiny knew exactly what happened but really didn't feel like talking about it. She also knew how she got there. She didn't, however, know that she was in Brockton because she wasn't paying attention last night. It didn't seem like they were driving that long. She thought about the ride and realized she had no idea how long they drove for.

Destiny turned her thoughts back to the present and hoped I hurried up before someone spotted her. She is still wearing the black dress she had on the night before. Her hair is no longer curled in most places. She figured she had to look a mess or like a prostitute. Destiny thought people would believe only a prostitute would be in the middle of the street, in the middle of the day, looking wrecked in an evening gown.

She also feared that her guest from last night would come looking for her. That thought didn't last long. She began thinking that they were probably glad she is gone so they wouldn't have to deal with the awkwardness of the whole situation. Then she thought that maybe it is just her that felt awkward.

When I got to Destiny, she was still crying. She is also still wearing the black dress from last night. Her hair is a mess and I feared the worse. The first thing I asked her is what is wrong and once again how she got all the way to Brockton. I asked several times but she didn't answer. We drove the rest of the time in silence until we almost reached Destiny's house. She spoke only then to ask for her cell phone.

Destiny damn near jumped out of the car before I stopped.

I was barely to her house. I said bye after her as she ran to the house. She never looked back and slammed her front door behind her. I was about to curse her and drive off. But I couldn't leave her in pain and alone when I know there is something wrong.

I turned the car off and went up to the door. I knocked several times but she didn't answer. I called out to her and she still didn't come back and open the door. I remembered that I have an emergency key to her house in my car. I went to my car, got the key, and let myself in.

Once inside, I found her lying on the bed crying. She was curled up in a ball, face down. I asked her if there is anything I could do? I asked her if a man left her stranded or if anything worse happened? "Because he can be dealt with." I added. She shook her head to assure me it was nothing like that. She only looked up to tell me she couldn't talk about it right now.

After that she buried her head back into her pillow. I asked her again to tell me what happened to her. She looked up again, glaring at me and told me to "please leave" in a stern voice. My mind said not to leave her because I knew something wasn't right. I looked at her for a few moments, hoping she would snap out of it and talk to me but she didn't so I left. I told her to call me later as I walked out the door.

I called Imani and filled her in on the details when I got back to my car.

"Mystery partly solved. I found Destiny." I told Imani. "Well actually she called me and asked me to pick her up. She was in Brockton. She didn't say anything to me about where she was or anything and she is acting really funny."

Imani asked, "Do you think someone drugged her, raped her or something?"

I told Imani, "I have no idea because Destiny is not talking to me at all. When I got to her house I went in to see if she was OK and she told me to leave. I am so scared for her."

Imani ranted on, saying she has to tell someone what happened in case she needs help or medical attention.

"How could she be so stupid?"

Imani paused all of a sudden. I was about to ask her what is wrong when she said that she thought she heard Jaloni's key in the door. A couple of minutes later Imani told me she would try to call Destiny later and that Jaloni is walking in the house and she hadn't properly wished him a Happy New Year. We said goodbye and hung up.

As soon as Imani came near Jaloni, the fight began.

"Are you deliberately trying to embarrass me or play me?"

Jaloni actually wanted to hold it in but as soon as he saw Imani it was all he could think about. He was tired of having the same arguments with Imani.

Imani just stood there with a dumbfounded look on her face. She had no idea what he was talking about. "Answer me!" He screamed. "Why do I have to get off the plane hearing about your episodes? You would think you could handle yourself more ladylike being a college educated professional. But like they say, "You can't take the hood out da hood rat!'"

"Go to hell Jaloni! I have no idea what you are talking about but you better watch your mouth!" Imani warned Jaloni as she glared at him.

"So you weren't fighting with some guy in the club, acting like a hood rat?" Jaloni asked with a smirk on his face.

"Why don't you ask me what happened? He disrespected me and jumped in my face and it is my episode? Why would you automatically assume I did something?"

"So you weren't trying to talk to his boy?" Jaloni asked looking very angry.

Jaloni really didn't want to know the answer to that question.

Imani shot Jaloni a shocked look and began to explain but when she looked at Jaloni she decided against it. She waved Jaloni off with her middle finger and stormed upstairs. She was thinking who could have possibly told Jaloni that. She had no idea but she wasn't going to admit it.

On the way up the stairs she warned Jaloni to worry about his episodes and hoes. That set him off again. He was screaming louder than before. "What hoes Imani? You always talking about my hoes but where are they? They aren't calling this house like your ex-Michael does. Where are they? I know you have checked my cell phone and two-way, were there any numbers? Do I hide like you do when I am on the phone? So who got hoes Imani?"

Imani chimed in with, "So why didn't you want me to come with you last night?"

Jaloni began to explain to her that he didn't want to be there either and he wanted her to enjoy New Year's Eve and not be stuck in a hotel room or at a basketball game. His face was relaxing now and his big brown eyes were no longer filled with anger. He announced that he knew he was going to be tired after the game and didn't want to disappoint her if he didn't feel like going out. She just glared back at him and kept going toward the bedroom.

About an hour later Imani came out of the bedroom and walked through the house looking for her keys. Jaloni had them in his hand. He got up and took them off the counter when he heard her coming out of the bedroom. He asked if she is looking for them, while dangling them around in his hand.

"Yes. May I have my keys please?" Imani replied in a dry annoyed tone. "I don't feel like playing games with you right now."

"Where are you going Imani?" he asked. "Damn I just got home today. Can't it wait?"

Imani shot back, "Wait like your accusations? Now you want to spend time with me? My friend is in trouble and I need to go see her. No! It can't wait."

"No I guess not; it doesn't matter that one of them is always in trouble or that I need you." He said as he threw the keys across the room.

"Once more, Jaloni, Go to Hell!" she told him as she went to pick up her keys.

When Imani got to the front door Jaloni was blocking it saying, "I'm sorry" over and over again. "Jaloni, I don't have time for this right now." Imani yelled at him and tried to move him from in front of the door. He picked her up into his arms and held her so tight she thought he was going to break something. She told him to stop and put her down but that only made him start kissing her. He kissed her on her face and then on her lips. He was still holding her tight. But now he held her up, off the ground with one arm.

He began unbuttoning her coat, then her shirt. She stopped fighting him. She knew she wasn't going anywhere. Jaloni was 6'9" and very strong. He could have held her up like that all day. When she stopped fighting he put her down and looked at her for what seemed like an eternity. She actually began to get nervous.

He didn't know what he would do without her. He shook that thought, knowing he didn't want to think of that right now. Right now all he wanted to think about was all the things he is

22

going to do to her. He reached over and started by popping her bra off from the front. He kissed her nipples and then he laid her on the floor, pulled down her skirt and looked at her once more before making love to her.

When she woke up, Jaloni was standing over her with a smile on his face. He said, "Happy New Year's" and grinned. She looked up at him wondering what happened to the angry man that greeted her earlier. Looking in his eyes she didn't see any of the anger. She removed the blanket he put around her while she slept and returned the sentiment.

After they made love again they talked. Apologizing for the things they said. Jaloni told Imani that he loved her so much and the thought of her talking to someone else is hard for him to handle.

"Do you want to be with someone else?" Jaloni asked.

He stared at Imani. In his mind, she was taking a long time to answer.

With a look of amazement on her face she exclaimed, "No Jaloni I don't! I want to be with you and only you."

"So why does it seem like we go through this so often if you're not looking for anything or anyone else?" Jaloni's confusion was written all over his face.

Imani looked at Jaloni and began rubbing him on his head and kissing him. She really didn't have the answer to his question.

CHAPTER 4

Destiny woke up the next night. At least she figured it was the next night. Destiny actually had no idea what time it is but she felt like she slept for a long time. She remembered me bringing her home but not much else. She thought back to me bringing her home and wondered if she told me anything. She didn't remember talking to me so she stopped worrying about that.

She realized that she was not dreaming about what happened on New Year's. She wished it was just a dream but the fact that she was still wearing the black dress she wore on New Year's Eve was a reality check. She thought about Imani and me. She knew she owed us some sort of explanation but she could never tell us about what happened or the feelings that she has.

Destiny thought that we would never understand and would probably treat her different. That's exactly why she would keep it to herself she thought.

Destiny felt so guilty about liking it. She also felt guilty about running out of Helena's house without saying goodbye. Destiny hates to admit that she enjoyed being with Helena. She has always had feelings for women but couldn't believe that she actually went through with being with one.

Helena's touch made Destiny feel alive. Destiny had never felt that way with any man. Even if it wasn't a wham-bam thank you ma'am, it still was not as stimulating as sex with Helena. Men didn't touch her like that. They only wanted to touch places that suited them or turned them on. She ran her past encounters through her mind to verify her thoughts.

Helena is fine too. Destiny had never thought about a type

of woman she would be attracted to but Helena is a no-brainer. She looks like a girl you would see in a music video except she carried herself with class. She has thick hips and supple breast. Helena's dark chocolate complexion shined. Destiny didn't realize exactly how beautiful Helena is until they got to her house.

Destiny couldn't help but to stare at Helena from head to toe when she stood before her. Destiny also liked the fact that Helena is feminine. Helena was in no way like the lesbians she has seen or is shown on television. Destiny was diving deep into her thought, remembering Helena's light brown eyes and how Helena stared deep into her eyes like she was reading her.

Destiny quickly snapped out of her thoughts, more confused than ever before. What is she talking about? She is not a lesbian. So why can't she get Helena off of her mind? Helena's face and body is etched in Destiny's mind. The things they did are also etched in her mind. Destiny is having a really hard time understanding her feelings. That's how she knew that no one else would understand.

Destiny thought back to high school. She had a crush on a girl in her class. She never said anything to the girl or mentioned it to anyone else. She did write about it in her diary. She later burned her diary to make sure that no one ever read it. The girl was a cute light-skinned girl with short curly hair. Destiny thought about befriending the girl and hanging out with her to see if anything could come out of it. Destiny never did because she was too scared and worried about someone finding out. She especially wouldn't have wanted her mother or me to find out.

Destiny also remembered that she had a minor crush on Imani when she first met her. She remembered being awed by Imani's beauty. The crush didn't last long and Destiny never told anyone about that either, especially not me. As Destiny developed a friendship with Imani the other feelings went away. Destiny also didn't think Imani carried herself in a way that accentuated her beauty, which also helped Destiny lose interest in Imani.

Destiny told herself it would never happen again. She had too much champagne and other things to drink. She thought to herself that the drinking made her vulnerable. She had to find a way to get the thoughts out of her mind.

She would call Imani and me tonight and make plans for the weekend. They would definitely want to go out man hunting. Yeah she will definitely be up for that. They will go out and she will find a man and all of the feelings she has for Helena will be gone.

I was starting to think and re-think about Darrell. Had I been too hard on him? I am wondering if he will call me again. The cockiness wasn't that bad, it was actually kind of cute. I like a man with confidence. He is so fine too. I remembered him smiling at me with his deep dimples just teasing me. He had to know that I was stressed at the time I said those things to him.

I am still worried about Destiny. I wonder if I will ever know exactly what happened to her on New Year's Eve. I just hope it isn't anything bad and that she is going to be OK. She is acting really weird and that is what is worrying me the most. Destiny has always been able to talk to me and she knows nothing will change the way I feel about her so I am wondering why she won't talk to me.

Destiny and I have been friends for a long time. We met in middle school and have been through a lot together. I began remembering when we double dated to the prom. We ended up leaving the prom with the limo because her date was acting like a jerk and my date thought it was funny.

After we left the prom we went out to eat at IHOP because we didn't want our parents to think anything was wrong. We took our time and didn't leave the restaurant until after midnight. Then when we returned to Destiny's house we sent the limo away.

My date called Destiny's house to inform us that they had no way to get home. I told him to take the T. He got so mad that he started yelling and cursing. I casually hung up the phone on him in mid-sentence. The memory of that night and the days that followed made me laugh out loud.

For the next week in school everyone laughed at them for getting dumped at the prom. Their comeback was they didn't want to be with us anyway. They tried to say they ditched us. No one believed them because they ended up stranded, asking for a ride home at the end of the night. Most people weren't going home and didn't want two extra guys hanging around killing their prom night action. The jokes continued until graduation.

My mind continued to drift, wondering if this year will be any different from last year. I have so much hope that my girls and I will find what we are looking for and do the things that make us happy. I was just about to call my mom when the phone rang.

It was Imani. "Hey girl, what are you doing? Jaloni was tripping. He said he heard about what happened in the club. Someone told him that I was trying to talk to a guy in the club. I want to know who told him that. It had to one of the guys working with your friend." Imani said before I even said hello.

I thought to myself, here we go.

Then she said, "Can you ask him who knows Jaloni?"

I told her about cursing Darrell out and informed her that I won't be asking him anything. She laughed and asked me why I cursed him out.

I told her, "I was worried about Destiny and tired and not in the mood to hear his BS. He was acting like he is all that and is only a bouncer." I continued, "Homeboy is fine though and I am sure that there are plenty women that would be proud to put up with the BS. I even had second thoughts about what I said to him because he is so fine."

Imani was laughing so loud she almost forgot why she called.

"So is Jaloni still mad?" I asked her to try to change the subject.

"No. He called me a hood rat and I almost lost it but I chilled and walked off. I came back downstairs to leave and check on Destiny, he blocked the door and apologized just the way I like." Imani asserted.

Imani then told me that she is still upset about the way he talked to her and she doesn't like when he talks to her like that and doesn't understand why he does it.

She continued by saying, "It really hurts my feelings because he says he loves me but is always talking down to me when he doesn't get his way."

Imani was ready to change the subject. She asked, "Have you heard from Destiny?"

I answered. "No."

Imani put me on hold and dialed Destiny's number. Destiny said hello and Imani bombarded her,

"Where did you go hoe? What's with you pulling that shit? Was it worth it? Why were you crying? How the hell did you get to Brockton?"

Destiny cut Imani off and said, "First of all, Denise had no right to tell you anything. I told her I was fine. Next time I won't call her to come get me because she apparently can't keep a secret. If I wanted it broadcasted I would have called the media."

Imani said, "Ewww!! You ungrateful bitch! I would have left your ass out in the middle of nowhere. How could you say that? She only told me because she is worried about you. Secret? What's so secret about that?"

I had to interrupt. "Stop it!! I can't believe you said that Destiny but it is OK because I won't come to get you anymore so you better make sure you always have a way home, someone to call, or at least know where you are instead of acting like you're crazy."

I thought Destiny's nerve was unbelievable. I quietly hung up the phone and took it off the hook. I'll let them argue it out.

CHAPTER 5

I am really not enjoying this year. It's feeling a lot like last year, except the drama is different. We were all supposed to be happy together, hanging out, finding our true loves, and getting into a little trouble. What's life without a little trouble? Boring! That is what my life is right now, boring.

I haven't heard from Imani or Destiny since we last spoke on the phone and I'm not going to call either one of them. I still can't believe Destiny. How could she even come at me like that? She must be crazy to think that was OK. I'm not stressing it though. I'll just know better next time.

I haven't heard from Darrell either. I think that is probably for the best. I know I don't need a man that thinks he is God's gift to women in my life. I need someone that knows I am his gift. So the question is why can't I get him off my mind? I truly felt something when he kissed me but I'm not sure what it is...

I thought about my mother, what she would have to say about all of this. I spoke to her on the phone a couple of times but I have not seen her yet this year. I think I'll stop by her house and see if she is at home. Hopefully she has cooked something to eat. I love my mom's cooking but thank God I don't eat there every day or I would be as big as the house. She's probably going to tell me that I am getting too skinny and over feed me as it is.

I walked in the door my mom looks at me and immediately asks, "What's wrong?"

I decided against telling her what was going on and told her nothing. She just looked at me and said.

"OK, but I know there is something wrong. I can always tell when there is something wrong."

I asked her if she has spoken to Destiny's mom and she said no.

"What you got to eat momma?" I asked.

She laughed and said "Whatever's bothering you can't be that bad. It hasn't affected your appetite yet."

We both laughed.

Then she asked me how Destiny is doing. I told her I didn't know and she gave me that "I told you so" look. She went in the kitchen to prepare me a plate of food and put it in the microwave. She just began to use the microwave a couple of months ago, although I gave it to her for Christmas three years ago. My brother, sister and I use it when we come over to heat up leftovers.

Momma got the plate and brought it to me after the microwave finished cooking it. She stands there, in front of the microwave, the whole time because she is afraid to leave it while it's cooking. She sat in her chair and began with one of her favorite speeches "You should be cooking for me; I'm getting too old to be slaving over a hot stove and those microwave dinners are the most flavorless things I've ever tasted."

I told her, "Momma, you know you would never eat my cooking. You don't eat anyone's cooking but your own. You'd be talking about my cooking like you're talking about the microwave dinners."

She shook her head up and down, laughing, not even trying to deny it. She is right though. Cooking is not one of my strongest traits. I was running around so much when I was younger I never took the time to learn how to cook. Who knew I would need it?

"So are you and Destiny talking to each other?" Momma asked.

I knew I couldn't keep her off the subject for long. She is like a dog with a bone. I pretended not to hear her and kept eating.

"I'll take that plate if you don't answer me." She said.

That definitely got my attention.

I answered quickly, "No momma we are not talking but I don't want to talk about it. Have you heard from Jr. and the children?"

"Yes I have. Why aren't you and Destiny talking, life is too short to not talk to someone over something trivial."

I explained to her that I couldn't make Destiny speak to me and that I didn't do anything to her but try to be a friend.

She said OK and left it alone, so I thought. "So you're not going to tell me what happened? Maybe I can shed some light on the situation. You want me to call her mother and see what she knows?"

I wanted to scream, "No" but politely shook my head no and decided it was time to leave.

When I got up to leave momma asked, "You're leaving already? You just got here."

I said, "I know and told her I have to run some errands. I will come back next week."

She smiled and said, "Don't forget about your momma." Like I could ever, she would call me until I came over.

Just as I got out the door my cell phone rang. "What are we doing tonight?" Imani screeched on the other end. "By the way, where are you? I tried calling your house and I got no answer."

"My, aren't you nosy?" I asked. She said, "Whatever hoe." I told her, "I just left my mom's house. Where do you want to go?"

She told me of an event being thrown by the Celtics and started telling me that she was going to hook me up with one of Jaloni's teammates. I thought she was joking because I don't date athletes so I said OK and we hung up.

I was just finishing my hair when Imani pulled up to my door. I came out the house and Imani yells,

"Uh-uh what is this? We are going to a party, not church." I had on a long black dress that showed nothing but let you know I had it to show.

"Don't hate 'cause you look like a hoochie." I yelled back and continued to the car.

The heifer locked the doors and was shaking her head no when I got to the car. I told her that if I go back in the house, I am going to stay there. Magically, the power locks opened and I got in the car. She told me I still look cute. Then she started telling me that Destiny is not answering any of her phone calls and how stank she was to say what she said to me. I just looked out the window. I didn't want to talk about Destiny anymore.

We got to the place and Jaloni was there with a guy who was taller than him. I thought to myself that Imani was not joking and I am in for a long night. He looked to be at least 6'11", a cute, chiseled face, light-complexion, and a magnificently cut body. Yes, I could tell that with his clothes on. The cream-colored sweater and blue leather pants he was wearing definitely did him justice.

He is a little light for my taste but picky is not in this year. I'm out to have fun. Jaloni introduced him as "The Future" and then said his name is Cliofus. Future looked at Jaloni like he committed a crime then turned to us and said, "You can call me Tyrone, everyone else does." He turned back to Jaloni and began

33

staring him down.

When we sat down to eat, I asked Tyrone if he lived in Boston. This must have been funny to Imani and Jaloni because they burst out laughing. Tyrone asked if I watched sports and I responded, "No I don't." as I rolled my eyes at Imani and Jaloni.

Tyrone let out a little laugh and said that is definitely cool with him, because that meant he could talk to me about other things. That made me smile. He began telling me about him, that he has just moved to Boston, after being traded here from The Los Angeles Clippers. He also told me that he is originally from Mississippi and is named after his grandfather.

Tyrone had the most luscious pair of lips I have ever seen. His lips combined with his deep sexy voice made me hang on his every word. He told me he would teach me about basketball if I wanted to learn and that I should come to some games. He would get me tickets anytime I wanted to come.

Imani interjected, "Please, I have been trying to get Denise to go to games for years. She only went to one game." She was about to continue but Jaloni put his hand over her mouth and kissed her when he took it away. Then Jaloni pulled Imani up and headed to the dance floor, leaving Tyrone and I to our conversation.

They came back to the table after a couple of songs and Imani played the early morning card. She told me Jaloni didn't drive his car so he was coming with her. She asked if I needed a ride or would I be alright with Tyrone. She was grinning from ear to ear and winking her eye. I told her I would be fine and said good night to Jaloni to alert her that he was already at the door. She told me to call her at work tomorrow to let her know I got home safely and winked once more before running to catch up with Jaloni. Then they were gone.

"Your friends are something else," Tyrone said after they left.

"Oh! My friends?" I questioned jokingly, "Don't try to deny Jaloni.

You know y'all are tight." We both laughed and then there was a brief silence.

Tyrone ended the silence, "What about you? What do you do?"

I told him, "I work for a public relation's firm but I dream of owning my own PR firm that deals mostly with minority-owned and startup companies."

He seemed very interested in what I said and I felt very comfortable with him. He asked a lot of questions. I liked that. He asked how I met Imani. I told him I met her in college and thought she was just another stuck up light-skinned sista until I got to know her. I was even more surprised to learn she was from the inner city of Boston.

I told him the story from the beginning when she came over and started talking to me like she already knew me. She had tickets to a concert that was being held on campus and asked me if I wanted to go. I thought she was going to give me the ticket but when I said I wanted to go she said cool and told me to meet her back there at 8 o'clock.

I came back to the student center at 8 but I wasn't sure that Imani was going to show up. I thought about it and wondered if Imani was one of those cliquey girls that would do something like that on a dare or for the sheer pleasure of seeing someone show up and wait. She did show up though and smiled a big grin when she saw me standing there. She then grabbed me by the arm and led me to the concert. I told him that I had a blast with Imani that night and how she even got us backstage with the band.

After the show she asked me if I wanted to go to breakfast with the band. We did and stayed until about 3:30 in the morning when Imani announced she was tired and asked the band member that was fawning over her to bring us back to campus. He was disappointed because he was hoping we were going to go back to their hotel with them but he told everyone we wanted to go.

When we got back to campus Imani gave me a big hug. She thanked me for coming with her and then she seemed to get sad. I asked her what was wrong. She told me that she enjoyed having a girlfriend to hang out with and that she didn't have any. She asked me if I would be her friend and we have been friends ever since.

He laughed. "That is an amazing story but it sounds like the Imani I met. Outgoing. So am I just another stuck up light-skinned brother?"

"Not with a name like Cliofus," I said laughing.

He looked shocked but started laughing also.

We talked for what seemed like hours. Actually it was hours because the owner came over to tell us he was closing the place. Tyrone asked for the bill but the owner waived him off, telling him it was taken care of and he could come back anytime. As we walked out the door the owner said, "Don't forget to bring the beautiful lady when you come back and good luck this season." Tyrone nodded and thanked the man for his hospitality.

Tyrone was a perfect gentleman at my front door. He told me he wants to kiss me but could wait if I didn't feel comfortable. I agreed with the waiting although I wanted to kiss those lips all night. The way I felt, who knows where that kiss would have taken us. Actually I knew, straight to my bed. Yeah, I believe waiting is a good thing.

We exchanged numbers. He gave me every single number he had. The home phone, cell phone, and two-way pager number with a code. Most men barely want to give you one number, I thought. After putting my information in his phone, he leaned over and kissed me on my cheek and then on my hand. He smiled and said good night. Yes it was, I thought as we said good night and I floated into the house.

CHAPTER 6

Destiny was at home reading a book when the phone rang. She looked at the caller ID to see if it was Imani or me. She still didn't want to deal with us and she still didn't have anything to tell us about New Year's Eve. She saw the number was blocked but she answered it anyway.

"Hello." Destiny answered the phone hesitantly. She was relieved that it wasn't Imani or me but she was a little surprised that it was Helena. Destiny didn't remember giving Helena her number. She kind of hoped that what they had was a one-night stand.

Destiny had to admit that she thought about Helena a lot, though. The smile quickly turned to a flurry of thoughts. She was so confused but didn't stress it. She wondered why Helena was calling her.

Helena asked, "Why did you leave like you did and where did you go?" Destiny told Helena, "I forgot I had an appointment and didn't want to wake you." Helena began to speak and Destiny interrupted, "I have never done anything like that before. I have never been with a woman and I am not a lesbian."

Helena responded, "I am not one either. I actually love men. I have been with women before but usually at a man's request or with one there. But when I saw you I just had to have you. I don't know what came over me. I just decided to cut out the middleman. No pun intended." She continued, "You don't know how surprised I was, and delighted you responded to me in the way that you did."

Helena explained to Destiny that she didn't call right away because she was worried about what Destiny would have thought.

Helena also told Destiny,

"I did want to call before to make sure you were OK and made it home safely but I was afraid. I hope you don't mind that I got your number from the phone book. I didn't think I would hear from you again and I decided that I wasn't OK with that."

Destiny thought to herself that she didn't plan on ever calling Helena. She really didn't have any intention of ever seeing her again. She felt telling Helena this would be rude so she kept it to herself. She actually had no idea of how this should be handled so she kept her mouth shut.

They continued to talk on the phone. Destiny found out they had a lot in common. Helena asked Destiny what she did for a living. Destiny told her that she is a nurse. Helena told Destiny that she was thinking of being a nurse and started the nursing program at her school. She explained that she had so much respect for Destiny because the program was too hard for her and that she changed her major to psychology.

They decided to hook up and go out on Saturday. Not a date or anything, just two friends hitting the town. Helena said that she knew of this club that would be perfect. She asked Destiny if that was all right. Destiny said that clubbing would be fine. They joked around for a little while longer then hung up.

The whole thing left Destiny with a smile on her face. If she can be friends with Helena then maybe what happened will never come up again. But how could she look at Helena and not remember what happened? She felt confused. Destiny was also disappointed that Helena only wanted to be friends.

Destiny wanted to cry but she wasn't quite sure why. She knew she didn't want to be in a relationship with a woman. She also knew that she had crossed a line she couldn't step back over. She tried to go back to reading her book but thoughts of Helena kept popping into her head. She closed the book and decided to go to sleep.

Destiny's phone rang again. This time Destiny picked it up, forgetting to check the caller ID. It was Imani with her usual abrasive speech.

"Where have you been, hoe? Why haven't you returned my phone calls, heifer? I can't believe you treated Denise like that. Well anyway, Denise and I are going out Saturday night because our men are going to be away and I wanted to know if you are going to be woman enough to put your differences behind you and come out with us."

Destiny told Imani, "I can't. I have plans. Imani flew off the handle, "Who are you going out with and where? Answer quickly because I think you are making it up." Destiny couldn't take anymore of Imani at that moment; she hung up the phone while Imani was still talking. Imani called back twice but only got the ring tone because Destiny didn't forget to check the Caller ID again.

Destiny began thinking about the last time we spoke. She realized that what she said to me was wrong but couldn't muster up the nerve to apologize. She thought about calling several times but just stared at the phone for a while before realizing that it wasn't the right time. Then she called a couple of times and hung up when I answered the phone because she was afraid that I wouldn't forgive her.

Destiny really wanted to talk to me about what was going on. She didn't know how to explain it or what exactly it was. Destiny even talked it out in the mirror but came up empty. She wasn't ready to tell anyone, especially not me. Destiny wasn't really sure if there is anything to tell. She kept telling herself that there isn't.

I was cooking dinner when Imani called me. She told me that she just spoke to Destiny on the phone. She also told me that Destiny hung up the phone on her. She explained that she tried to get Destiny to come out with us on Saturday, leaving out the part about cursing her out. She told me that she attempted to call Destiny back after and that she didn't answer the phone.

"Destiny is acting so stank." Imani said in an aggravated voice.

My response to Imani was. "Where are we going on Saturday? We haven't made any plans."

Imani proudly stated, "I knew we would because Jaloni and Tyrone will be out of town. I thought that Destiny would want to come and make up to you for the way she acted."

She changed the subject, telling me that she heard there is a new club opening downtown and she needed the release because playing wifey is too hard. She said, "C'mon," continuously until I finally gave in.

She said, "Cool. I'm driving and wear something appropriate for the club this time. Bye."

"Bye Imani." I said with a laugh on the tip of my tongue.

I just sat and breathed as I usually had to when I hung up from talking with Imani. I had to shake my head. Imani was too much but I loved her dearly. She keeps me on my toes.

The phone rang again. I picked it up and said hello. I could hear the person breathing and I let them know I could hear them breathing. After I said hello a couple more times the person hung up. I went to the other room and checked the caller ID but the number was blocked. Oh well I thought if it is important they will call back.

Two minutes later the phone rang again. I walked over to the phone and saw that the number was blocked so I decided to let the answering machine get it. Someone sighed and hung up. I didn't recognize who it could be. I thought it was weird but went back to preparing dinner.

I was watching TV later and someone called again and once again the number was blocked. Once again I walked away from the phone and decided to let the machine answer it. This time it was Tyrone. When I heard his voice I rushed back over to pick up the phone.

I answered the phone completely out of breath, "Hello baby."

He asked, "Are you busy?"

I said, "No. I just wasn't near the phone."

His next question shocked me.

"Baby do you want to come with me on Saturday? The game is in New Orleans and I am going home to Mississippi on Sunday. You can meet my mom."

"Isn't it a bit soon to meet your mother?" I asked.

His reply was. "No not at all and I always run women I planned to be serious with by my mother."

I thought damn momma's boy but said, "I'm sorry. I promised Imani that I would keep her company while Jaloni is out of town, maybe next time."

He said, "OK."

Tyrone sounded so disappointed that I wanted to change

my mind. He said good night, telling me he just called to ask me that.

"I have an early practice and I fly out in the afternoon. Do you know how much I'm going to miss you?"

I answered. "I do if it is close to how much I am going to miss you."

I laughed to myself, thinking how corny I have become since Tyrone and I started dating.

That made my night. I never thought I would meet a decent basketball player. Although being around him is making me want to kill his gentleman act. A sista has needs and he looks like he could take care of all of them. We have fooled around but he has always stopped short of going all the way. Even when I drop hints that he can go further he still stops, saying that he should go home.

Then I thought about what he said. He wants to get serious with me. What does that mean? Have we been going out long enough for things to be serious? I guess that explains a lot. I guess he figured that he could get sex from anyone but wanted to get to know me before we took it there. I was truly impressed. The thoughts that went through my mind led to sleep with a big smile on my face.

CHAPTER 7

I was looking good and feeling good. But Imani was looking exceptional and ready to play. She had on a genie-type outfit that was a long corset top and sheer pants. The pants could be tied at the bottom to give a genie affect but Imani wore them untied. This left them slit all the way up her legs.

This outfit is all that she has on under her coat. I could say nothing but damn when she took her coat off.

"I thought we were going to the club, not the Playboy mansion." I said looking Imani up and down.

She tried to play it off, "What? I have on clothes. Furthermore this outfit would kill Hugh Hefner."

We both laughed.

I felt totally overdressed. I had on a black scoop neck top and some tight-fitting black leather pants and black high heel boots. When I took off my jacket she asked, "Who died?"

I shot back at her, "Apparently Jaloni but if he hasn't, he will when he sees that outfit."

Imani rolled her eyes. The look that she gave me let me know that she didn't want to hear about Jaloni tonight. I began to laugh but she just kept walking toward the club.

I saw that Darrell was at the door as we got close to the club. He was looking just as good as I remembered. He stopped me to give me a hug, he let go and asked if we could talk. Imani started in on him. "Isn't your boss going to be mad at you for fraternizing with the patrons? Move along and go bounce someone."

Imani looked at Darrell as if she was angry with him or something.

I didn't understand why she was looking at him like she was but I did not question it. Imani then pulled me away from Darrell. Darrell looked at me like he was embarrassed or confused but didn't say anything to me. He just nodded his head up and down and turned away. I kept looking back at Darrell wondering what the whole episode was about. I also looked back and shrugged when I saw him looking to let him know that I had nothing to do with Imani's treatment.

The club's atmosphere was cool. It was a different environment than the other clubs around the area. The crowd was mature and laid back, more so than the clubs we usually went to. I was glad I dressed the way I did. Imani got a lot of disapproving stares, even from men. She was the only woman that was provocatively dressed in the club and she stood out. This has probably never happened to her before.

Imani began noticing the glares and decided she wanted to go into the VIP area. The bouncer at the door wouldn't let us into the VIP area. Imani was about to begin cursing at the bouncer when Darrell came up and told the bouncer that it was OK to let us in the VIP room. Darrell Stated "They are Jaloni's and Tyrone's girls. They're cool."

Imani turned to Darrell, who was staring at me, and said "Thanks" in a dry annoyed voice and then she pulled me away from Darrell.

Imani liked the fact that Jaloni's name could get her into places but not that everyone knew who she is. I never understood that. Most women would gladly announce being a ball player's girlfriend. I personally don't care whether or not people know that I am with Tyrone. Hopefully that knowledge will make a woman think first before approaching him.

Imani smiled a devious grin at the bouncer before we went

in the VIP room. The bouncer moved the barrier and we went in the room. The view was no different in the VIP. It was a dim room with blue lights. There were a lot of professional people in the room. There were no athletes or celebrities. The music was a mix of Jazz and Neo-Soul.

Some people were laid back on the couches and chairs listening to the grooves. There were some people on the floor getting their step on. I've always thought that stepping was cool but R. Kelly really put it on the map with his stepping song. People can be seen doing it everywhere.

I began wondering about Darrell and why he was staring at me but not saying anything. If he has something to say to me he should just say it. I doubt there was anything other than hi that he could have to say to me. I know Imani is acting stank toward him but he doesn't have to pay her any attention.

When I looked around, Imani had found some approval. She was in the corner with a man. Upon closer look I realized that the man was white. This made me curious so I headed in their direction. When I walked up she introduced him as Paul and said he worked with her. She took my showing up as her excuse to leave, saying that I am ready to go. I looked at Imani because I wasn't ready to leave but I followed her lead as she rushed from the room.

Imani didn't say anything all the way home except bye when I got out of the car. I didn't even bother asking her what was wrong because I know I would have gotten "nothing" for an answer. So I said bye and got out of the car. I looked back as I headed toward my house. Imani was still parked when I got to my front door. I thought this was weird because she usually speeds off when she drops me off.

My mind was on calling Tyrone so I didn't pry. I care about what is bothering Imani. I also wanted to make sure he got to Mississippi OK. I called his cell phone and a woman answered. I was about to get excited or hang up but something in my mind told me not to. Lucky for me, I didn't because it was his mother. I heard him in the background asking her who it is. She asked who I am and upon my answer her voice lit up.

"How are you, baby? Tyrone told me all about you. He says you're smart, beautiful, and ambitious and not ambitious for his money like a lot of these women out here. When are you coming down here to the swamps to visit us?" she continued, "We don't see Clio that often so I hope next time he comes he'll bring you. He'll be right to the phone. He is just drying the dishes."

I smiled to myself. My NBA man is drying dishes. When he answered the phone I said,

"Hello Clio."

He said, "Ha-ha. I miss you."

"Why don't you like the name Clio? I think it is cute. Can I call you Clio?" I asked in a cutesy voice.

He said yes and changed the subject.

"So what did the girls do tonight? Did you get into any trouble?" I was surprised he asked that. Jaloni must be telling him stories.

"Why would you think I would get into trouble?" I asked.

He exclaimed that he has seen more than his share of women out without their men and they can get pretty rowdy. He was laughing the whole time so I knew there are no worries.

Tyrone and I talked on the phone for more than an hour and he didn't even want to hang up then. It took a lot of persuasion on my part to get him to hang up. I was tired and a little worried about Imani. He also had to be up early in the morning to go back to meet the team. They had a game in Atlanta on Monday so his time was limited.

I was drifting asleep happy, thinking about Tyrone when the phone rang. I answered and a familiar voice was on the other end. Not familiar enough for me to recognize but it was a familiar voice.

"Hey, beautiful." The voice said.

I knew it wasn't Tyrone so I asked, "Who is this?"

"It's me Darrell. Don't you remember my voice?" He answered. "I was just calling to see if you got home OK."

"Yes I did. Why wouldn't I have?" I whispered.

A whisper is all I could manage.

"Do you know what time it is?"

He asked, "4 a.m. Why are you whispering? Am I interrupting something?"

"My sleep is what you are interrupting." I answered.

I really hoped that he would get the message.

I couldn't believe how he said the time nonchalantly like he was someone on the street that I asked for the time. He had to know I meant did he know how late he was calling me. Darrell continued by asking me if I had fun at the club?

I answered, "Yes."

He said "Good."

Darrell then started asking me generic stuff about the club. He asked, "Did you like the atmosphere, the music, did you meet any men?" He stopped himself and said, "Oh yeah you wouldn't be looking for anyone since you are Future's girl now."

I wanted to ask how he knew that but I know how small Boston is so instead I is. So instead I asked him if there is a purpose for this phone call. I know he didn't call me at four in the morning to do a phone survey about the club.

"Why are you asking me so many questions about the club?" I asked. I was a little annoyed at the questions and at the fact that he called me so late.

I was beginning to think that maybe Imani wasn't paranoid and that he could be where Jaloni gets his information. Then I thought to myself that I was beginning to become paranoid like Imani. Darrell's answer to my question shocked me.

"A brother has to know if his investment is going to pay off." Darrell answered.

I could practically see him grinning through the phone.

"Do you own that club or are you promoting for someone?" I asked.

I asked Darrell this because I know a lot of people that promote for club owners or are given a night but it's not their own. Some of them talk like they own the club so I was trying to distinguish. I was beginning to wake up because I was curious to hear the answer.

"Yep, I own it. That is the reason I haven't called you. I actually opened one just like it in Atlanta in February. Maybe one day I can take a friend to see it."

"A friend huh" I answered. "Don't you have plenty of them?"

Darrell sucked his teeth and told me that he hasn't been able to think of anyone else since New Year's and that he knew right away that I was the woman he wants to marry. He explained the reason he came on so strong is that he wanted me to feel it too. I have actually thought about him also. Even though things are good between Tyrone and me, Darrell sneaks in my mind every now and then.

"If you were thinking about me you would have found time to call."
I began, "I would have found the time if I was thinking about
someone."

"I know, but when you cursed me out I thought maybe you weren't
interested and then I get back in town and sources tell me that you
are dating Future and I definitely knew I didn't have a shot." Then
he slyly snuck in. "Do I have a shot?"

Darrell's whole voice and mood changed when he continued
talking, "You know what? You don't have to answer that. I messed
up and I'll live with it. Sorry I woke you or interrupted you. Take
care beautiful."

He hung up before I could say good night or anything else.

After the conversation with Darrell, I couldn't get back to
sleep. I began thinking about his weird behavior earlier and how
our conversation ended. I was also thinking about the things he
said. He knows I am the woman he wants to marry? He doesn't
even know me that well. We haven't even talked a lot since we met.

I shrugged it off as a usual line of BS that men give women,
figuring the quickest way to a woman's drawers is to bring up
marriage. He probably figures that I am around the age that
women began to get "desperate" for marriage. He has probably
used that line on many women. It has probably worked for him
also. I am not the one. I am not desperate to get married. I am
happy right where I am.

Darrell telling me about the nightclubs didn't impress me
either. Men are always thinking they have to impress me
materially. They don't realize that it doesn't impress me. I am
interested in how Darrell could possibly afford to buy two
nightclubs in two different cities. He probably told me about the

nightclubs, assuming it would put him in the picture and change things.

Nothing has changed in my mind. Tyrone is so good to me and wants to be serious with me. It has nothing to do with the money Tyrone makes. It's all about how happy Tyrone makes me. I smiled, thinking about Tyrone as I tried to regain my sleep.

CHAPTER 8

Destiny and Helena went out and everything was cool. Neither of them mentioned New Year's Eve or what happened between them. There were no uncomfortable feelings, just two friends hanging out. They spent most of the time joking around, singing with the songs on the radio. Helena took Destiny to a club in Rhode Island that Destiny hasn't been to before.

Destiny figured this club is cool because she always ran into the same people when she went out with Imani and me. She was anxious to see some new faces and possibly meet some new people, especially new men. She knew nobody in this club. It felt good to not have people in the club know you or know of you. She also thought that the chance of her running into an ex or someone that knows an ex was also slim here. She could tell by the look of the crowd that none of those people would hang out here.

The people in the club were extremely friendly and the atmosphere was different from any of the other clubs Destiny has been to. There were a lot of people dancing. The people appeared to be dancing in large groups but they didn't seem snobbish or cliquey. Men and women were coming up to her saying hello. Destiny felt so comfortable in this club, she had to smile.

Destiny eventually struck up a conversation with one of the guys that standing near her. He was cute, about 5'8", slender built with a light skinned. Not the type of guy Destiny is attractive to or talks to but he was definitely nice looking. They talked for a while and realized they were both from Massachusetts. He introduced himself and they decided that they would keep in touch. Randall asked Destiny to dance and she gladly accepted.

They danced through a couple of songs and Helena came

over. "Oh, there you are Destiny. Hi Randall. Glad to see you guys are hitting it off." Destiny thought nothing of this except that Helena was happy she found someone to dance with. Shortly after Helena walked off, Randall said he had to use the restroom and left Destiny on the dance floor. That was the last Destiny would see of either of them until the end of the night.

Destiny didn't think this was weird but gave up hope of him coming back. She chalked it up as another chance meeting and went about her business. She was curious about Helena though. She wondered why Helena wanted to bring her here if she wasn't going to spend any time with her. Destiny understood about them just being friends but thought it was rude of Helena to just leave her alone for most of the night in a place that is unfamiliar to her.

Helena came up to Destiny at the end of the night and nearly leaped into her arms. She asked if Destiny had fun. Destiny looked around to see if anyone saw this. She thought people would get the wrong impression if they saw that. Helena proceeded to tell Destiny about plans to go back to a friend's house for an after party. "Randall is going to be there. It seems like you two hit it off." She said smiling from ear to ear. Come on, you have to come! It'll be fun! You can sleep tomorrow."

Randall came up and asked if he could ride with them because his roommate was going ahead to straighten up the place. Helena said. "Cool." Helena grabbed both him and Destiny by the hand and headed out the club hand in hand.

In the car Destiny and Randall continued to talk. She was really enjoying his company. He asked her what she did for work and she told him she is a nurse. Randall told Destiny that he is a grad student that is studying psychology. She laughed when he told her the human mind excites him.

The whole drive Helena smiled and laughed a couple of times but she didn't join in the conversation. Destiny knew she was listening because she laughed at the right moments. At one point Destiny began to wonder what was on Helena's mind but only asked if she enjoyed herself at the club tonight.

Upon entering the apartment Destiny noticed groups of people making out. She noticed an abundance of same sex couples and threesomes. She looked over at Helena who took her by the arm and rushed her through the room to another room where there weren't as many people but the same activities going on.

Randall reappeared and came directly to her. He sat next to her and wrapped his arm around her shoulder. At that moment Helena got up and left. She wondered where Helena was going. Destiny also wondered if Helena was going to participate in any of the activities. She remembered Helena talking about being in threesomes in the past.

Randall and Destiny talked for what seemed to be a long time. Destiny really felt a connection with Randall but couldn't keep her mind or her eyes off of the activities that were going on around her. She thought Randall must have noticed that she was uncomfortable because he asked her if she wanted to go to his bedroom. He told her that there was nobody in there and he promised to be a gentleman.

They talked a little more in his room and then he kissed her. Normally she would have backed away from kissing on the first meeting but in a way she felt she had something to prove to herself since being with Helena. She was also feeling the affects of being surrounded by people making out. They kissed for a while and then Randall began undressing her. She didn't stop him. She wanted him too and began undressing him.

He got up to take what was left of his clothes off and Destiny looked at him, all of him and she was definitely turned on.

She could feel herself throbbing, lovin' it. This must definitely mean she is not gay. After about ten minutes she pulled him on top of her and shifted around until he was inside of her.

The door opened just as she was getting into it. It was Helena. Uh oh Destiny thought but she couldn't stop and he didn't stop. They were both too far into it. Helena said, "Sorry for interrupting." She had a big smile on her face and was blushing. She began to close the door but Randall invited her to stay with a wave of his hand.

Helena didn't hesitate to jump on the offer. She came in the room and watched for a couple of minutes before she got undressed. Destiny didn't realize that Helena got undressed because she was so into what she and Randall were doing. The next thing Destiny knew Helena was on top of her, sitting right over her face. She then stuck her fingers in Destiny's mouth and asked if she liked the taste.

Helena then began to fondle Destiny's breast and Destiny couldn't take it anymore. She started screaming and shaking. Randall pulled out but Destiny didn't even notice until Helena went down on her. Destiny began screaming and moaning even louder and as her head turned she could see Randall in the corner watching and smiling.

That's when it hit Destiny that she had been played. When Destiny came down from the high she was feeling, she came down hard. Once again her guilt returned. Why was she feeling this way towards a woman? She has feelings for men. She looked at Helena and began to get angry. Helena came over and tried to comfort her and Destiny lost it.

"You set me up! You knew I wouldn't sleep with you again so you used him to get to me. I should beat your ass!"

"What are you talking about?" Helena responded, "Randall is the one that invited me to stay and when I didn't hear any objection from you. I just thought..."

Helena stopped trying to explain and stormed out of the room. Helena kept going, running out the apartment.

Destiny was left to find her way home once again. This time Destiny didn't know who to call or exactly where she is. Destiny asked Randall to take her home but he said he didn't have a car. Randall also offered no other solution and acted like he really didn't want to talk to Destiny. At first Destiny thought this to be weird. Then it made perfect sense. It confirmed that Helena set up the whole episode.

It was almost 4 in the morning but she left Randall's apartment anyway. There was definitely no bus service and she didn't know how she would get home. Destiny wouldn't get on a bus in her condition anyway. Once again she was stranded. She tried to call Helena but she either shut her cell phone off or just wasn't answering it.

Destiny decided to walk around and see if she recognized anything. She didn't. With no one to call, Destiny kept walking. Destiny did a lot of thinking while she walked. She knew she would have to face whatever is going on inside of her and deal with it. So that's what she decided to do while she walked.

Destiny finally found a train station at 6:15 in the morning. She walked for over two hours not including the time she sat on the bench at a bus stop and just tried to get her mind right. She got home around seven thirty and Destiny showered like she was on the street for days. She thought about everything that has happened to her the whole time.

What would her mother say? What would her friends think? She then realized she didn't have any friends. Imani and I were pretty much all the friends she has and she has totally alienated us. Then there was Helena who she realized is not her friend at all. She tried to sleep when she got out of the shower but couldn't calm down enough to sleep.

I answered the phone and could hardly hear the person on the other end say hello. I yelled hello again and knew it was Destiny. "Who is this?" I asked.

Destiny hung up the phone. I called Destiny back and the phone rang for a long time. The answering machine picked up and I yelled that I was going to call an ambulance if Destiny didn't say something.

Destiny picked up and said, "I'm so sorry." she continued. "I missed you so much."

"Why are you calling now Destiny?" I asked. "Why didn't you call and apologize when it first happened?" She responded by saying she was going through a lot and couldn't talk about it fully until she totally understood. She asked me to forgive her and be patient with her.

"So there's nothing I can help you with?" I inquired. She answered no and asked if we could be friends again one day.

I told her, "Yes. Always."

She managed to get a little laughter out through the crying. I told her to take care and that I had to go and hung up the phone.

Destiny was pleased that I said we could be friends. She still didn't know what to tell me about what she was going through. She also didn't know how. Destiny resorted back to her original plan of telling no one anything about it. She decided that there was really no reason to tell anyone now anyway. It is definitely over between her and Helena. Destiny didn't even want to be friends with Helena after last night.

Destiny wondered how she could be so stupid. She should have known that Helena has no boundaries from the discussions they had on the phone. Destiny got into her bed and pulled her covers all the way up over her head. She promised herself that she would be more selective about who she deals with in the future.

CHAPTER 9

The Celtics didn't make the playoffs this year so Tyrone decided to go home for a while. He invited me down to Mississippi, telling me I would have his full attention because there was no basketball to think about. This time I accepted his offer. We made the plans to leave on Saturday afternoon. I was to stay a week with Tyrone and his family. I am actually looking forward to meeting his family and getting to know the people that are important in his life.

Mississippi is so different than Boston. He lived in a small town outside of Biloxi. It is May so the heat and humidity is almost overwhelming. The sunshine is beautiful. Thank God for the trees because the sun is blazing hot. There were no clouds so you could see the blue skies for miles.

The nights are amazingly beautiful. You can see the clear sky and the noise of crickets is a relaxing change from car horns and construction equipment. I spent most of my time at night outside because Tyrone's mother didn't believe in air conditioning. I also spent a lot of time outside because Tyrone's mother didn't like my "siditty Yankee ass." Yes, that is a direct quote.

Tyrone's mother almost blew a gasket when I said I only want one child and to run my own business. "Who is going to take care of this child while you are off playing businesswoman?" This is another direct quote from his mother. Tyrone looked so embarrassed and kept apologizing to me for his mother's behavior. He didn't once try to defend me or tell her to stop. But what can a man do when his momma is the one talking about his girlfriend.

We spent most of the days away from the house also. He took me to New Orleans and to different parts of Mississippi. He also took me to his high school to see his jersey and championship banners that hung in the gym.

Tyrone got a lot of attention in Mississippi. He is like a hero here. He explained to me that people very seldom left Mississippi and that many of the basketball players have the talent but don't make it as far as he has. He also said some of them didn't want to because it meant leaving. He also told me that the people like having someone represent to their area and it felt like having the whole area on his shoulders at times. He explained that they are watching and praying he didn't mess up.

We were there for three days when I began to feel like I couldn't take it anymore. Tyrone came out to see if I was OK. He woke up, went by my bedroom, and realized I wasn't there. Yes she had us in separate bedrooms.

"I thought you caught the first thing that moves and headed out of here." He laughed.

His smile went away really quick when he realized I wasn't smiling with him.

"Don't worry about her. The only one that has to approve of you is me and I do." He said looking very serious.

"Why didn't you tell her that?" I asked.

He said, "It doesn't matter and if I did she would have only gotten worse."

He told me, "I don't understand it. She never acted like that towards anyone else I brought home.

"Anyone else? How many women have you brought home Tyrone?" I had to ask.

"Two. I brought my first girlfriend and my ex-wife." He said and looked up quickly to see my reaction.

"Ex-wife? You never mentioned having a wife. Do you have any children? Is there anything else you want to tell me?"

"I have two children. One is 17 months and the other is 3 years old. The only reason I didn't tell you is because I didn't know when the right time was or that we were going to get this serious. I'm an athlete. I can't just tell anyone my business. I have to make sure I can trust them. You could have called my wife or alerted the media or anything. I have had that done to me in the past." And his rant went on.

When he finally finished I told him that I noticed he called her his wife twice in his speech and he just shook his head.

"We are not divorced yet and sometimes I don't know if I want to be divorced. She is strong and independent and didn't want to leave her career every time I got traded. She also didn't like what she saw behind the scenes. Some of these NBA men are trifling." He admitted.

"Yeah! Some of them. Would any of them be the ones that lead people to believe they are single and that they have a future with them?" I shot back at him. I continued by asking, "So is that why your mother doesn't like me? She thinks I am just like your wife?"

Tyrone shrugged his shoulders at my question. He really didn't know why his mother didn't like me.

I demanded Tyrone take me to the airport and he did without an argument. There was silence in the car for the whole drive to the airport. Tyrone kept watching me, looking for an opportunity to speak. I don't know what I would have done if he did speak. He wanted to wait with me and talk everything over at the airport. I just wanted him gone. He told me he loves me and I nearly exploded. I remembered that I was in a public place but I couldn't hold it in.

"Why don't you go home and tell your wife you love her you sick bastard? Don't ever say that to me again! Don't call me! Don't ask about me! Forget you ever met me dickhead!" I screamed.

He looked around to see if anyone recognized him and I burst out laughing.

"Hey Cliofus, what's the matter? Scared someone may alert the media that there is yet another trifling Negro in the NBA? Nobody cares about that. Just keep scoring every night. I mean on the court in case you are confused."

He ran up to me and tried to quiet and hold me and I screamed bloody murder.

A couple of police officers came and asked if everything is OK. Tyrone told them that he and his wife were just talking. He turned to me with a pleading look.

"I am not his wife; I am his mistress." I screamed.

One of the cops snickered but regained his composure quickly. Tyrone put his finger over his mouth to quiet me but it only pissed me off.

"Shhh!!!! You weren't Shhh'ing me when I was screaming your name out in bed or when I asked you all of the questions you lied to me about."

The cop interjected and told me I would have to quiet down or I would be asked to leave. I quietly asked the cop to remove Tyrone from the airport and they did. The one that was snickering recognized Tyrone and asked him for an autograph as they took him away. I thought that was so funny, I burst out laughing. Tyrone looked around bewildered to see what I was laughing at. He saw nothing funny so he turned back to the officer and signed the autograph.

I sat at the airport and was devastated. I couldn't believe he lied like that. But why couldn't I believe it? That is the reason I never wanted to date an athlete. I ought to call Jaloni and Imani and give them a piece of my mind for setting me up with that loser.

Then I thought to myself that he is not the one who is a loser, I am. I couldn't do anything but sit and think about it. My flight isn't for six hours. I truly thought about calling Imani, waking her ass up but I didn't. I am so hurt I can hardly breathe.

A man sat near me and attempted to begin a conversation with me. I really wasn't in the mood to talk to anyone so I ignored him. He didn't like that and began mumbling something under his breath. My first instinct was to curse him out with all the anger I have pinned up in me. I didn't and he eventually got up and walked off.

Sometime during the night I must have fell asleep because I was awaken by an airport employee that gave me a first-class ticket and a letter. The letter was from Tyrone. It said he is sorry and the ticket was first class because I am a first-class lady that should have never been treated the way he treated me.

He went on to say he is confused and I am the first woman that made him think of leaving his wife. He explained that everyone else he met was one night stand material or even if more, definitely not marriage material. He said he will regret his decision not to be honest with me forever and asked for my forgiveness.

I threw the letter in the trash but took the ticket. I am no fool. The flight to Boston is over 3 hours long and I would have had to wait for an open flight because this was not my departure date. I shook my head as the letter landed. I couldn't believe Tyrone's gall. He admitted that I am not the only woman that he has cheated on with his wife with but expects me to believe that it would be different with me.

I thought a lot about the situation with Tyrone during the flight home. I asked myself what I did to deserve this. I searched through my memories and couldn't find anything that would lead me to believe I deserve this. I have never lied to or cheated on anyone. I've played my share of games but nothing on this level. I'm sure everyone has played games to a certain extent.

I thought about his mother. She was so happy to talk to me on the phone and ask when I was coming down, knowing full well that her son is married. I really think she, as a woman, should have said something to me. I began to wonder if her attitude towards me was her way of trying to get rid of me. She knew full well that I work and that I am ambitious because she told me so when I talked to her on the phone.

I wonder if she feels guilty at all or is she just another one of those mothers that will support their son even if they know he is wrong. She probably thought I knew and is just one of those females that didn't care because he is a basketball player. I stopped trying to figure his mother out and turned my thoughts back to me.

The next thing I thought about is why I never thought to ask him if he is married before. I am always the one that is so careful and thinking I would never get caught up in a situation like this because I can see the signs. Thinking back, the only reason I could think of is I got too caught up in Tyrone and the thought of being in love. I was so quick to say he is a good man because he has a good job and makes a lot of money. I also thought he was a good man because he didn't do the obvious things like rushing to have sex with me.

I made a mental note to thoroughly interview and investigate any man I go out with from now on. I'm going to be so careful and question everything. Men are going to think I am the FBI but if they have a problem with it or honesty, they can move on. I decided that I wouldn't be going out with anyone, anytime soon. I'll take time off to shake the bitterness I am bound to feel from this experience.

CHAPTER 10

Helena called Destiny every day since the incident but Destiny would not answer her calls. Destiny did a lot of thinking but was still confused about the whole Helena situation. She knew she liked Helena and being with Helena but she didn't want to be labeled or thought of as a lesbian. She also didn't like the fact that Helena set her up. Destiny thought that if she wanted to be with her, she should have been up front with her about it.

Destiny finally broke down and spoke to Helena. Helena started by explaining that she was very sorry and didn't realize what happened would hurt Destiny so much.

"I thought you were cool with it when you came to the club. Most people know about club Premiere and what goes on there. If I knew you didn't know, I would have told you." Helena exclaimed. Helena continued by telling Destiny she would never take advantage of anyone, especially someone like her.

Helena paused after her admissions but got tired of waiting for Destiny to answer after about the third one.

"How long am I going to have to beg for your forgiveness?" Helena was responding to Destiny's silence. "I know it's not going to be too much longer because I am about to stop. I said I am sorry."

Destiny didn't say anything because she didn't know what to say. She couldn't believe Helena took her to a swingers club and thought she would be OK with it. Destiny thought how dumb she was not to realize what was going on in the club as well as at Randall's house.

"Destiny!" Helena's yelling brought Destiny out of her thought.

At this point Helena was really frustrated by Destiny's silence. She didn't mean to yell at Destiny but she did want to know if Destiny was going to forgive her.

"What Helena?" Destiny answered.

She hadn't heard a word that Helena said.

"I am just wondering what you could have possibly been thinking. Why would you take me to a place like that?" Destiny continued. "So essentially, you are admitting that you set me up?"

"I didn't set you up. Yeah I wanted you but I had nothing to do with Randall." Helena answered. "Like I said that night, if you would have objected I would have left the room."

Destiny could tell she was lying as she ran the night through her memory but she let it go.

"Are we cool? I'll never put you out there like that again. I'm so sorry." Helena's voice changed and she sounded wounded. "I just want us to be friends and I'll do it on your terms from now on."

Destiny thought for a moment and said, "OK. Whatever Helena."

Helena sighed loudly on the phone in relief.

"Are we starting over?" Helena asked.

Destiny's response was, "Yes."

Helena asked to meet Destiny for dinner. Destiny agreed and they made the plans before hanging up.

Destiny and I have spoken a lot in the past weeks. She seems to have changed a lot. There is definitely something going on with her. She seems unfocused and tightlipped. Sometimes I feel like I am talking to a stranger. She still hasn't told me what is bothering her. If I ask her what is wrong she gives me a quick "nothing" for an answer and changes the subject.

We made plans to go to dinner tonight. She asked me not to tell Imani or invite her. I told her that was fine and that I hadn't heard from Imani that often since I got back from Mississippi. I told her that I get the feeling that Imani is trying to avoid me to keep the peace with Jaloni. Destiny just laughed at that.

I explained to Destiny about the conversation Imani and I had. I told her, "By the time I told Imani what happened, she had already heard Tyrone's version from Jaloni. Of course Tyrone told him I made a scene in the airport and in his version, he is totally separated from his wife."

I filled Destiny in about Jaloni's rampage. "He told Imani he couldn't believe her ghetto friend did that and for her to never ask him to hook any of her friends up again. She told me he is always calling us ghetto and talking down at her when he gets mad. My response to Imani was to check Jaloni because the only reason he is not still in the ghetto is because he can play basketball. He is not above anyone. Imani said she knew but changed the subject."

Destiny began laughing again.

"So you got ghetto?" she asked.

"I did not. Since when you know me to be ghetto?" I asked.

Jaloni's whole reasoning had me shaking my head. I couldn't help but laugh as I thought back at the scene in the airport though.

"Come on Denise. You can tell me. Was your neck snapping back and forth while you waved your hands in the air at Tyrone? Were you sucking your teeth?"

Destiny was having so much fun with this. She was cracking herself up. I reminded her that Jaloni called her ghetto too.

Destiny responded, "I know I am ghetto. There's no need for me to worry about Jaloni saying it. Why are you worried about him saying it about you? Truth hurts?"

I told Destiny to go to hell and that I would see her tonight. She was still laughing loudly when I hung up the phone.

It was actually good to hear Destiny laughing. It's been a while since I have heard her laugh like that. I just don't like the fact that she is laughing at my expense. I am not ghetto and Jaloni is lucky he doesn't have the guts to say it in my face or I would tell him about himself. I was still thinking about it while I was looking for something to wear to dinner.

I got to the restaurant early. A woman appeared to be following Destiny when she came into the restaurant. The woman was still with her as she approached the table. I hardly heard the introduction because I was staring at the woman. I snapped out of it when she extended her hand to me for a handshake.

I apologized for not hearing her name, telling her that I lost my train of thought for a second. So she caught me up to speed, telling me her name was Helena. I was a little out of it still as I shook Helena's hand. I am also wondering why Destiny didn't mention she was bringing someone else was coming to dinner.

We sat down to dinner and the conversation was like a voyage of our past. It seems almost like Destiny is telling Helena her life story. After we ordered, Helena got up and excused herself. Destiny's first words after Helena left the table were, "Well? What do you think of her?"

"I guess she is OK, why do you ask?" I answered.

I was getting more confused about what is going on.

Destiny got serious and told me that Helena and she have been going out. She told me she met Helena on New Year's Eve. I just looked at Destiny with total confusion. Destiny's smile disappeared when she saw my face. "Don't look at me like that."

Destiny then told me that she is not a lesbian but Helena makes her happy. I had nothing to say but a million questions were running through my mind.

"So she is the one that left you in the middle of the street on New Year's?" I started.

"No. I ran out of her house. I was scared, embarrassed, and confused when I woke up next to her." She said, interrupting me "She went out to look for me as soon as she woke up. Please try to understand this, Denise."

The rest of the dinner I got to know Destiny's "girlfriend." Apparently so did Destiny. Every time I said really. Destiny said really. I got the distinct impression that Destiny did not know Helena very well at all. Helena's phone rang and she excused herself to answer it. That was a good thing because it gave me the opportunity to ask Destiny what was going on.

Destiny was smiling; grinning would be a better word for it, until I asked her about not knowing anything about Helena. She angrily told me that Helena is not her girlfriend, they are just friends and she reminded me that she is not a lesbian.

"So? Why the big production?" I asked. "You bring her here, ask me if I like her, tell me how happy she makes you and then turn around and say she is not your girlfriend? What is going on with you?"

"We're just having fun." Destiny stated in a matter-of-fact voice. "She makes me feel good. We hang out sometime and go to parties and sometimes we have sex. It's not a relationship."

Shaking my head, I said, "OK. Destiny, if you are in a relationship with this girl you can tell me. It won't change anything between us."

Destiny coldly answered, "I don't care if it would. I already told you I am not in a relationship with her. We are friends. I wouldn't need your approval. I just thought it would be great for two of my friends to meet."

Helena comes back to the table and gives Destiny a kiss on the mouth. She wraps her arms around her neck, saying. "Baby I have to go. You and your friend enjoy the rest of your dinner and I will talk to you later." Helena turned to me and smiled and said goodbye and she was out the door.

Destiny just looked at me.

"What is wrong?" I asked.

"I'm sorry I snapped at you. The truth is I like Helena so much but I am so confused. I have feelings for men. I am attracted to men. I have been with a man since I began seeing Helena and its fine with her. We even had a threesome that started off with this guy I met at a club and her joining in after I was already aroused. I am not a lesbian and she says she is not either. There is just something about her, something I have never felt before."

I didn't know what to say. I just looked at Destiny and grabbed her by the hand. She looked like she is awaiting a speech. I was stuck on the threesome but definitely had nothing to say about Destiny's situation. Whatever makes her happy is alright with me.

For the rest of the evening we talked about everything but Helena and their relationship. Destiny asked me about New Orleans, telling me she always wanted to visit during Mardi Gras. She also asked why no one, including nosy ass Imani, thought to ask Tyrone if he was married. "That is the least she could do before she forced him on you." Destiny said. I was just silent and decided it is my turn to ban a subject from dinner.

Destiny asked about what is going on with Imani and

Jaloni. "Don't you think it is strange that Imani is taking Jaloni's garbage?" I had no answer to Destiny's question. I didn't want to get into that either or discuss it. I have no right to judge anyone's relationship after what I have been through. I was happy when the check came because it has been one unusual night. I paid the check, kissed Destiny on the cheek and headed for the door.

Once outside, Destiny asked me what I was doing for the rest of the night. I told her I have some work I brought home to catch up on. She looked disappointed but said OK. We said goodbye once again and Destiny reached out and hugged me tight.

I thought about calling Imani and filling her in on what happened tonight, see what she thought of it. I also wanted an answer about why no one thought to ask Tyrone about being married. I quickly thought against calling Imani. I didn't want this situation to get any more dramatic than it already is and I have decided that I am going to forget about Tyrone and what happened with him altogether.

CHAPTER 11

Imani was just reaching her desk when the flowers arrived. This is the sixth bouquet in the past three weeks. She doesn't know who is sending them and it bothered her so much. Jaloni got upset when she asked him about the flowers, ranting about her sleeping around and asking about who she is messing around with. Imani asked Jaloni if he thought she would be dumb enough to ask him about the flowers if she were sleeping around. Jaloni just rolled his eyes and walked off without answering. Imani shook her head in amazement.

She always asked Jaloni not to send her flowers at work but she thought she would ask him anyway. Imani explained to Jaloni that she is a private person and she didn't like the fact that people took flowers as an open opportunity to get in her business. People who don't even usually speak, come around when she has flowers on the desk, asking, "Who they are from? What's the occasion? Or something that is none of their business."

That is exactly what is happening to Imani right now. One of her co-workers is at her desk saying,

"You deserve a man that spoils you. I like the way your face lights up when the flowers come in. It's nice to see you smile."

Paul continued by asking her if she had been back to The Twist. That was the club where he saw her for the first time outside of work and fell in love with her.

"Paul, these flowers are not from my boyfriend. I don't know who they are from." She whispered.

"You mean your man is not sending them?" Paul asked slyly.

He knew the answer to the question because he is the one sending the flowers.

"How do you know I have a man Paul?" Imani inquired. Paul shook his head in disbelief at Imani's inquiry.

"I just figured someone as beautiful as you would have a man in her life. If I didn't think so I would have asked you out a long time ago."

Paul smiled a nervous smile when he said that because the last part slipped out. Imani just looked at Paul, not knowing exactly what to say to his admission. She began smiling nervously back at Paul because she didn't want him to think she was totally rejecting him. Men don't handle rejection well and she didn't want any drama at work.

Later that night Imani called me and told me about the flowers and what Paul said to her. We went through a long list of who could have sent the flowers and came up empty.

She then said, "I thought perhaps it is Jaloni playing with me or trying to be romantic. But he got so angry and began accusing me of sleeping around so I know they are not from him."

I thought to myself that he wouldn't take it that far if he sent them. I feel Jaloni has been disrespecting Imani far too often but instead kept it to myself. She could deal with that in her own way, on her own time.

"Did you try calling the florist?" I asked breaking the silence.

She said, "Yes. The florist said the person paid good money to remain anonymous. Denise, this is scaring me! What if this person is stalking me? He knows where I work. I can't get any support from Jaloni because he thinks I brought it on myself."

I almost slipped and said something about Jaloni. He was unbelievable! I wonder if he thinks that he is bringing it on himself when those groupies are throwing themselves at him.

I told Imani, "Please be careful and I hope the person is either revealed or goes away."

She said, "OK goodbye."

Imani explained to me that Jaloni would be home soon and if he sees her on the phone he'll start in on her and she did not want to hear it.

I was still thinking about Imani's situation after I hung up with her. The situation with the flowers scares me but the situation with Jaloni scares me more. She is scared to be on the phone when he is around. She seems scared all the time and that's no way to live. I hope she figures that out before it is too late. I also hope it is not too late. Imani never mentioned anything about Jaloni hitting her but there is definitely something wrong there.

CHAPTER 12

Destiny is on the phone with Helena, trying to explain why she brought me to dinner when they were supposed to be going out. Destiny explained to Helena that she wanted me to meet her because I was one of her oldest and dearest friends. Helena didn't buy it for a minute and she let Destiny know it.

"If you didn't want to go out with me why didn't you just say so? Helena asked Destiny, interrupting her explanation.

Destiny continued with her story. "I did want to go. I just thought it would be a good idea if you met Denise."

"Why?" Helena asked skeptically.

"I told you. She is one of my best friends and I thought it would be nice for you two to meet." Destiny wasn't sure why either.

"Next time just say that you don't want to go or be alone with me. Nobody is trying to force you." Helena answered.

"I'm not lying to you Helena! That's your way of handling and doing things, not mine." Destiny answered angrily.

She was really getting tired of Helena's attitude and accusations.

"I get it Destiny. You are not a lesbian; you don't want to be in a relationship with a woman. I wish you would be honest with yourself about what you are feeling so you can start being honest with me." Helena's tone matched Destiny's annoyance level.

Helena tried to talk to Destiny but she really wasn't feeling it anymore. Helena also didn't want to keep talking to Destiny because she knew she is getting nowhere with her and is beginning to fall for her. She was pissed she felt this way about Destiny but hoped that she would come around.

"I have to go. I'll talk to you later." Helena told Destiny.

"Helena." Destiny started but didn't say anything else.

"What Destiny?" Helena answered.

Helena really hoped that Destiny had something profound to say like she loves her or something to hang on by.

"Nothing. I was just going to say good night." Destiny answered. She did have something she wanted to ask Helena but couldn't get it out.

"When am I going to hear from you again?" Destiny asked.

She shocked herself with that question.

Helena was shocked too but she kept her cool.

"I don't know. When I get some time. I have a lot of things to do." Helena answered Destiny coldly.

"OK." Destiny said sadly. "Goodbye Helena."

Destiny slammed down the phone.

Destiny's attitude perplexed Helena. She wondered what Destiny's problem was. Helena thought about it and began to feel a little guilty about coming off so cold to Destiny. She really didn't know how else to handle her. All Helena wanted was for Destiny to take her seriously and possibly consider a relationship with her.

Destiny and Helena's conversation saddened and confused her. She couldn't understand why Helena took that tone with her. She thought about it and decided it is just the way Helena is. She already knew Helena is a person who would do anything to get what she wants so why should it surprise her that she began to get hostile with her.

Destiny called me on the phone to see what I am up to and if I had any plans for the weekend. When I answered the phone, I was a little shocked that Destiny is on the other end. I hadn't spoken to her in weeks. When I answered the phone I could tell something is wrong with her although she tried to hide it.

Destiny said, "Hey girl, what have you been up to? I haven't heard from you in a while. What you got a man over there keeping you busy?" She sounded overly chipper. That is another indication that something is wrong.

"Naw ain't no man here. I told you I gave up on those." I answered her laughing.

"Yeah, right! You'll never do that. I know I would never do it." Destiny said. She was laughing harder than I was and continued. "What are you doing this weekend? I was thinking we could hang out on Saturday night. How's Imani?"

I told her, "It's been a while since I spoke to Imani." I also told her about Imani receiving flowers at work and Jaloni flipping on her for it.

"How is it her fault if she doesn't know who is sending them? I said. "Sometimes I don't understand men or why we put up with them."

"She has no idea who sent them? She didn't meet some guy in a club, on the street, or in her office building? You know Imani is friendly everywhere." Destiny said as she started laughing again.

"It's not funny because it's scaring her." I answered Destiny's last remark in a sharp tone.

"It's not that serious. If someone wanted to hurt Imani they would have done it already. Damn! You need to go find your sense of humor." Destiny's answer was just as sharp as mine.

"I'm sorry Destiny. I am just worried about her. Because of the flowers and because of how Jaloni is acting toward her. I really don't know which one is worst." I said to Destiny realizing that I shouldn't have taken my feelings out on her.

Destiny continued, Don't to worry. Imani will figure it out. It has to be someone she is overlooking sending her the flowers." She also assured me that they are probably harmless, saying that a person that is spending that much money is not out to hurt Imani. I thought about it and figured Destiny was right. The person hasn't even confronted Imani to the best of my knowledge. I'm probably worrying for nothing.

"We have to go out and get you a man." Destiny began talking again.

"What? Why we got to get me a man?" I asked her. I was very curious to hear her answer.

"First of all, you are up here worrying about Imani's problems more than Imani. Secondly, you are coming up with all types of conspiracy theories for her problems." Destiny answered. Once again she was right. About me overanalyzing Imani's problems, that is.

"How is a man going to change that?" I asked Destiny. "A man might make me more paranoid." I began laughing but Destiny didn't.

"I'm only joking." I thought I should say that in case Destiny thought I am serious.

"Oh I know. I am just thinking about Imani and Jaloni and I think it is about time he put his foot down with her. She takes full advantage of him." Destiny stated. She was so matter of fact about it I began to think that it may be true.

"That's not true. She doesn't take advantage of Jaloni." I answered.

Destiny laughed and said, "OK, if you say so."

I decided to change the subject so I asked Destiny how Helena is doing. Her answer is that Helena is mad at her and she doesn't know why. She told me, "Helena asked why I invited you to the restaurant the other night. I think Helena wants more than I can give her so I am going to stop seeing her."

I asked Destiny, "How do you know Helena wants more?" She didn't have an answer. She said, "I just got a feeling." I left it at that. I didn't know anything about how women deal with each other. I also didn't ask her why she didn't want more with Helena. It was a road that I rather not journey down.

Destiny called Helena back after hanging up with me. Helena wasn't going to pick up the phone but she was curious to see what Destiny wanted. Destiny asked if Helena was surprised to hear from her.

"Frankly. Yes. Why are you calling?" Helena asked Destiny.

"Come over." Destiny told Helena.

"I'm not falling for that. Why do you want me to come over?" Helena asked.

"I think we should talk about our friendship, get a better understanding of what we expect out of it." Destiny said in a chipper tone.

This was starting to worry Helena so she told Destiny, "I don't expect anything out of our friendship."

"OK, so just come over. I'm sure we can find something to do."

Destiny said it but she didn't know why.

"I'm not coming over there. There is nothing there for me." Helena answered.

"Please. I promise you there is something here for you." Destiny told Helena.

Helena finally agreed to come over. She hoped that Destiny wasn't playing games because she is not in the mood for it. She got in her car and the whole drive there she asked herself why she is doing this. She thought that although she is falling for Destiny she is no one's fool. If Destiny is not acting right when she got there, she would leave right away.

Destiny answered the door in a see-through teddy. Helena began to talk but Destiny put her finger over Helena's mouth. Helena wasn't sure about this but Destiny looked too good and she wasn't going to say no to that.

Destiny told Helena to undress. Helena obeyed. She stared at Destiny the whole time, partly because she thought she was being tricked and partly because Destiny looked amazing. When Helena undressed Destiny came to her.

"Do you want me?" Destiny asked.

Helena didn't answer. She just stood there looking at Destiny.

Destiny asked her again, "Do you want me?"

Helena said, "Yes."

Destiny answered her, "Take me then."

Helena shot Destiny a surprised look. She started to talk again and Destiny kissed her on the lips. Helena was very confused by Destiny's actions but thought she would play along. Destiny began rubbing Helena's body with her index fingers and it began to stress Helena out.

Destiny led Helena into the bedroom and pushed her on the bed. She straddled Helena and asked her what she wanted from her.

"For you to stop playing games with me, Destiny." Helena answered Destiny's question.

"Done." Destiny said and kissed Helena again. "From now on there is no games, just you and me like this." Helena wasn't sure what that meant but at that moment it sounded good to her. Helena laid back and let Destiny take charge. Destiny started touching and kissing Helena all over. Helena got excited but wanted to see if Destiny would go all the way. She pushed Destiny's head down toward her pelvic area and got no resistance. Helena laid back again and let Destiny do her thing.

Helena was shocked that Destiny went through with it without protest. She was used to being the one that did the pleasing when she is with Destiny. She is still skeptical about Destiny's motives but right now she would just enjoy being with Destiny.

She pulled Destiny back up face level by her hair. When Destiny was face to face with her she looked into her eyes. She didn't see any anger or fear. Destiny kissed Helena hard and began fondling her breast. Helena returned the favor. She touched Destiny's breast and then stuck a finger in her to see if Destiny was really turned on. She was and Helena was finally convinced that Destiny really wanted her.

After they finished making love, Helena tried to talk to Destiny again. Again, Destiny shh'ed her and told her they are good. "No strings attached right? Friends?" Destiny asked Helena.

Helena knew there was a catch. She went along with Destiny.

"Yeah. Friends." Helena told Destiny.

"You said we are going to do this on my terms. My terms are we are nothing but friends and that no one is to know anything about it. If you agree we can do this anytime we want." Destiny told Helena.

"So that is what this is about? Your friend was grossed out?" Helena asked.

"No she said she is OK with whatever makes me happy." Destiny answered.

"So do you want the secrecy?" Helena asked.

"We aren't lesbians right? I'm not and you told me you are not. So what is the use of parading around together like we are?" Destiny responded to Helena's question. She smiled at Helena, letting her know those were her terms.

Helena said, "Yeah, no problem." Helena thought to herself that there is a problem, a big problem; she is in love with Destiny.

"Good now come over here and give me some more." Destiny said with a laugh. She was so relieved that Helena agreed to her terms.

Helena reluctantly had sex with Destiny again. This time Destiny was totally uninhibited. Helena wasn't. Helena didn't want to enjoy it because she knew her feelings were involved. She went through the motions but she wasn't aroused. Destiny either didn't notice or didn't care. She was just wrapped up in the moment and exploring Helena's body.

Helena got right up and got dressed when they were done. She didn't say anything to Destiny until Destiny asked her why she is in such a rush.

"I have to finish up some work at home. I almost forgot about it. I'll call you." Helena answered.

"OK. Thanks Helena. When will I see you again?" Destiny asked. "And don't give me that busy line either."

"I don't know Destiny. I'll let you know." Helena responded as she was halfway out the door. She closed the door before she finished talking.

Helena was so mad at Destiny. She couldn't believe the only way she could have her is if she kept it a secret. She began wondering why Destiny wanted it secret all of a sudden. Helena didn't know if she could handle being with Destiny under those terms. She looked back at the house before she got into her car and drove off.

CHAPTER 13

For the first time in a long time Destiny, Imani, and myself are hanging out together. It took a lot of work on my part to get both of them to come. It took two weeks but I finally found a day that both of them are free. Destiny is busy exploring the, her words not mine, relationship with Helena. Imani is busy trying to please Jaloni and stay out of trouble to keep the peace. Those were also Imani's words. She called it playing "Wifey."

I suggested we go to The Twist. At first, Imani was not too thrilled about going there. She started saying that someone that works with Darrell is probably still watching her, telling Jaloni things. She came around without much convincing, saying she needed to see different faces and Jaloni is out of town anyway.

I was kind of disappointed when I got to the door and Darrell wasn't there. We went in and it was just like I remember. This club definitely has a smooth feel to it. There were no hoochies, wearing almost nothing, running around trying to get attention. Even Imani had scaled down her dress code for the night. She had on a fitted shirt that exposed one shoulder and leather pants. She also seemed different.

The first opportunity I got I asked Imani what was wrong.

Imani's response was "Nothing."

So I tried, "My! Aren't you over dressed tonight?"

She looked at me and smiled. She didn't respond with her usual, "Go to hell heifer, Fuck you hoe," just a smile and a nod. That was all I got and she appeared to be forcing that. I asked her again what is wrong and that if she told nothing I would keep asking her until she answered.

"I'm just toning it down. Jaloni told me that if I want him or any man to marry me I have to change the way I am. I thought about it and he is right." Imani said in a matter-of-fact tone.

"He is not right. The person that marries you will accept you for who you are. This quiet, reserved person is not you." I interjected.

She began telling me that his mother said she was too rough around the edges and not good for his image.

"Image?" I was screaming now. "NBA players have images? They are the most trifling...."

I stopped myself because I was getting personal and realized that was more about Tyrone. It's not fair to Jaloni to lump him in with the rest of them. Having a stank attitude is the only thing I know him to be guilty of.

I told Imani I am going to the bar to get a drink and asked her if she wanted one. Imani just nodded and gave me the fake smile again. I didn't even bother to ask if she is sure she is OK. I wasn't really going to get a drink anyway so I was glad that she didn't want one. I was going to look for Darrell. Don't ask me why but I was.

I asked one of the guys I remembered seeing with him before where he was. I was shocked and a little disappointed to learn he moved to Atlanta. I left a message about the club being great and how I wish him all the success with his ventures. The guy promised to tell him, saying he'll probably call in tonight.

I walked back to the area where Imani was sitting. Before I got there I noticed this fine dark skin man trying to talk to Imani. She wasn't her usual flirtatious self. She was barely looking at the man. The man finally gave up and walked off. I sat down and asked her what that was about and she said, "Nothing." "Did you see that man Imani? He is fine." I questioned. She answered yeah she saw him but he isn't her type. I got no smile, no cocky yeah I could have pulled him look. Imani was definitely not herself but I am done asking her about it.

As we sat there a drink came to me from a "Secret Admirer." It's a Cosmo so the person has to know me or have been watching me. I don't usually take drinks but I took the drink thinking Destiny is playing a prank on me. Then I began wondering where she went. I had not seen her since shortly after we came in the door. I told Imani that I am going to look for Destiny and she said nothing, just sat there.

I looked almost everywhere for Destiny. I bumped into her as I walked past the restroom. For some reason I didn't think she came out of the Ladies room but I left it alone. I was about to ask where she had been when a guy came out of the restroom and tapped her on cheek and said goodbye. I glared at her but didn't say anything. She gave me a weird look and asked Imani's whereabouts.

I told Destiny Imani is sitting in the corner. Destiny laughed and asked if Jaloni put her on punishment. I just glared at Destiny and asked her not to say that around Imani. "Oh now we can't say anything about her situation but she never hesitated to rub our nose in ours or make us feel small? I'm damn sure not going to hold my tongue for her. She never did for me or you." Destiny shouted.

I was going to say something but I just left it at that.

The bartender came over and asked me my name. I asked why and he told me there is a phone call for me at the bar if my name is Denise. I got scared, wondering if something happened to a family member or something bad. I didn't even think how anyone in my family would know I am here. I ran to the phone and said hello, sounding out of breath.

"Hello beautiful. I heard you are gracing my club with your beauty tonight. What do I owe the honor? Did you enjoy the Cosmo?"

"So you are the one that sent the drink? How did you know I liked

Cosmos?" I asked before I told him, "It's girl's night out and we were having some fun."

He laughed and answered, "I figured you were a Sex in the City type girl. That's cool that you guys have a girl's night out, just don't tear my place up like you almost did the place on New Year's Eve."

I laughed. There was silence and I guess he couldn't hold it anymore because he asked about Tyrone. I told him I didn't know where he is and I could almost feel him smiling through the phone.

"So you two got into an argument?" He asked trying to make sure it wasn't temporary.

"No. No argument." I protested, "Just an understanding that we weren't meant to be together."

There was more silence and finally I spoke. "Atlanta? Or should I say Hotlanta huh? What made you leave and when did you leave?"

He told me the club in Atlanta needed more attention and the neighborhood where it is located is in turmoil so he needed to find alternative ways to get people in the club.

"The women must be treating you right down there?" I jokingly asked.

He said, "What women? I gave up on women when I realized that I couldn't have you."

On that note, I told him I had to go find my friends and I wished him well. I told Darrell that he could call if he needed a friend to talk to any time. I said goodbye and handed the phone back to the bartender. I could feel myself blushing so I rushed away before the bartender could notice.

Talking to Darrell made me smile. The smile disappeared quickly as I walked through a crowd of people that emerged near the spot I left Imani. I was worried about Imani and hoped nothing happened to her. I got closer and found Imani and Destiny fighting. People were just watching, not even trying to break it up. I shoved through the crowd and a chick shoved me back. I couldn't worry about that now.

I got to them and pulled Imani off of Destiny. Imani looked up and smiled. The first real smile I saw from her all night. "I have wanted to do that for a long time." Imani said and headed back towards Destiny. Destiny tried to retaliate and Imani yelled, "Come on!" in an almost demonic voice. Destiny backed up and looked at her before walking off.

The guy I saw coming out of the bathroom with her followed her out the club. I knew it would be impossible to get an answer out of either of them about what happened but I asked Imani anyway. She fixed her clothes and hair and sat back down like nothing happened.

"Am I really that crude? Do I rub everyone the wrong way?" she asked.

I asked her, "What are you talking about? Why would you ask that?"

Destiny told Imani that Jaloni is right and nobody wants to be married to a loudmouth slut. She told me Destiny called her crude and told her Jaloni and everyone sees it. Imani apologized to me for slugging Destiny. She said she didn't know what came over her, it was like she snapped. "I'll apologize to Destiny."

When she finished talking Imani went right back into the trance she was in earlier. Some people walked by, asking if she is OK. Some people were just staring at her. I thought about Darrell telling me not to tear his club up. I had to smile but none of this is funny. I asked Imani if she is ready to go and she said, "Yes please." I asked if she could drive and she said yes but didn't look like she could so I took her keys from her.

Imani was quiet the whole way home. She just looked out the window. She spoke her first words as I headed to my car. "Don't leave me." I looked at her, bewildered. She said it again, "Don't leave me." I tried to tell her that she would be OK and Jaloni would be home soon. She said she didn't want to be alone with him or in this house. I got close enough to hug her and tell her good night and she wouldn't let me go. She started mumbling that she is sorry for everything and then she passed out.

CHAPTER 14

Imani woke to the news of her miscarriage. She was torn between the thought of almost having a baby and being happy she wasn't having a baby with Jaloni right now.

"How are you doing?" I asked Imani, noticing her mind was somewhere else.

She nodded to tell me she is OK so I continued.

"I tried to call Jaloni but he didn't pick up the phone. I tried his cell phone and got the same result."

She said, "It's OK. Don't call him anymore."

She also had a request. "Can you help me find a place to live and help me move my things out of Jaloni's house when I get out of the hospital?"

I said, "Yes of course but why?" I was truly surprised by Imani's request.

"I've known for some time that our relationship is going nowhere. I just didn't want to face it. Thank you for not saying anything about the way he was treating me. I love you."

That is all she could manage to say before she drifted back to sleep.

Imani woke up the next morning and couldn't believe her eyes. Her hospital room looked like a florist. There were roses of every color. She had never seen so many flowers in one place before, except in the movies. She was truly amazed at them but she is also worried because I am the only one that knows she is in the hospital.

Imani buzzed the nurse, mostly because she didn't know what else to do. She asked the nurse to find the card for the flowers so she could thank the person or people. After looking through all of the bouquets, the nurse told Imani she couldn't find a card. She asked if there is any way to find out who brought them.

The nurse went to the desk and got the desk nurse. The desk nurse saw the man and had a description. She said he came with the delivery man about nine this morning. She told Imani he was about six feet tall, green eyes and brunette with short spikes in the front. She also said he was very well dressed with an athletic build and slightly bowlegged.

Imani said, "Paul!"

The nurse asked in an envious tone, "You know him? He said he will be back to see you later." Imani shook her head up and down then glared out the window. She began wondering how Paul knew she is in the hospital. It is Sunday so no one at work would have known.

When Imani woke in the afternoon she was about to use the phone to call me but was startled when she looked around and saw Paul sitting in her room. She was also a little worried but couldn't manage to say anything. She reached for the nurse button and Paul leaped toward her.

"What do you need? I'll get it for you. How are you doing?"

She finally spoke, "Paul, how did you know I was in the hospital?"

He told her he saw what happened in the club and followed her car to her house to make sure she got home OK.

He continued, "I know Denise is your friend but I wanted to make sure they weren't setting you up or anything like that. The other girl looked very mad when she left. I pulled up to your house just as you collapsed. Are you OK?"

Imani shook her head yes, deciding against telling Paul why she was in the hospital. She didn't want it getting around work.

"Why didn't you tell me you were the one sending me the flowers?" She asked. "You saw how bewildered I was about receiving the flowers and you never said a word? Why?"

Paul turned around like he was shocked.

"Who told you?" He started. "I know I am not your type; I just like to see your face when you get them. It lights up and you are so pretty."

He answered and looked at Imani like he was seeing her for the first time. She is so pretty, even with no makeup Paul thought Imani is stunningly beautiful. He thought about it and remembered that Imani isn't much of a makeup wearer anyway.

Paul came back to reality and told Imani that he is sorry for not telling her about the flowers.

He asked Imani, "Maybe we can be friends?" Paul smiled nervously, mostly because he didn't know what else to say or do. He never thought she would find out about the flowers. He thought in his mind that possibly the room full of roses may have been a little much. As he scanned around the room he agreed with himself, yeah they are definitely too much.

Imani looked back at Paul and decided he is harmless.

She answered. "We can definitely be friends but one thing."

Paul looked puzzled until she said, "No more flowers. It was a sweet gesture and I appreciated the flowers. I just don't like to the scene that flowers cause."

He said, "Deal. Maybe we could go out to lunch sometime?"

She said. "Yes that would be cool."

Imani and Paul talked for almost an hour until Jaloni came in the door. He didn't even say hello or ask how Imani is doing. He just started in on her.

"What happened to you?" Jaloni asked while looking at the chart like he could read it.

Imani answered, "I am fine. I just fainted because I am under a lot of stress."

"What stress? All you do is work and hang out with your friends. What were you and your friends doing that caused you to pass out?"

Imani looked at Jaloni, she couldn't believe his reaction. She could be dying and he is in her hospital room acting like she did something to herself. This is exactly why she knows it is time to leave Jaloni. Jaloni looked down at Imani after she didn't answer. He then picked up the chart and looked at it again. He was getting more and more frustrated that he couldn't read it.

Paul was shocked to see Jaloni Johnson standing in Imani's room. He wondered if Jaloni was her boyfriend. Imani never admitted to having a boyfriend and got upset when he assumed she has one Paul thought. He also wondered why Jaloni is so angry. Paul knew nothing positive could come out of him staying so he decided to go.

As Paul made his move to leave when Jaloni turned and saw him. Jaloni gave Paul the meanest look Paul had seen in his life but didn't speak. He just stared at Paul like he thought Paul was going to say something to him. Paul actually thought about saying something to Jaloni because he didn't understand his aggravation. He thought Jaloni thought that he was too good to have his, whatever interrupted by Imani being in the hospital. Jaloni stood up tall as he could, to show Paul how big and tall he actually is. Paul knew Jaloni did this to intimidate him. Paul rushed out of the room without looking at Jaloni again or saying goodbye to Imani.

Paul's mind was stuck on that scene. He wondered if Jaloni is the reason Imani didn't smile at work and if he is abusing her. He thought about getting a guard or doctor to go to Imani's hospital room but then thought against it. He figured Jaloni couldn't do any damage to Imani while she is in the hospital.

Jaloni turned his attention back to Imani when Paul left and began asking questions again.

"Who's that Imani?"

Imani stared at Jaloni for a long time then answered him hesitantly. "That is Paul. He works with me. He is also the one that has been sending me the flowers." She pointed to the flowers as she talked to Jaloni.

"Really?" Jaloni asked slyly. "What was he doing here? How come he knew you were in the hospital but I didn't?"

Imani answered Jaloni. "I don't know. He was here when I woke up. You didn't answer your phone. I don't feel like talking about this right now."

She knew Jaloni well enough to know no answer is going to be the right one. She was sick of answering to Jaloni anyway.

Imani asked Jaloni to get the doctor for her. After staring at her for what seemed like an eternity he finally went out to the nurse's station and told them Imani wanted a doctor. After going to the nurse's station, Jaloni returned to Imani's room and just stood there staring at Imani. Only then did he think to ask her if she was OK.

Just as she began to answer Jaloni, the doctor came into the room. The doctor asked Imani if she was OK. She nodded that she was but shifted her eyes towards Jaloni. She told the doctor she felt a little pain. It was true but she wasn't in enough pain to require a doctor. She just wanted to talk about her information and ask them not to tell Jaloni anything.

The doctor asked if Jaloni could leave for a moment after recognizing Imani's signal. Jaloni asked the doctor why he had to leave. The doctor stared at Jaloni without answering until Jaloni put his head down and walked out the door. After Jaloni left, Imani demanded that no one give Jaloni any information on her condition.

The doctor asked if Jaloni caused the miscarriage. She answered no and told the doctor he was out of town. The doctor also asked her if she is being abused and questioned her about the bruises she had on her body. He made sure Imani knew there are resources available if he is and she wants to get out of the situation. She told him that Jaloni would never put his hand on her and about the incident in the nightclub. He changed the subject back to her information being private then reminded her about needing rest.

The doctor reiterated that Imani needed rest when he saw Jaloni going back into the room. Jaloni first told the doctor that he just wanted to talk to her and see what is wrong. He explained that he is worried because he just came back into town and she is in the hospital. Jaloni opened the door to Imani's room and looked at Imani who was facing the window and closed the door and began to follow the doctor.

Jaloni continued to follow the doctor down the hallway, pressing him for answers. He was becoming enraged because nobody would give him any answers. "How come I can't get any information? I come back from playing a game to a message on my voice mail saying Imani is in the hospital and I come here and get treated like a stranger. That is my life in there." Jaloni's yelling and rage fueled the doctor's suspicions.

The doctor began to question Jaloni about the bruises on Imani's body. "Bruises? What bruises?" Jaloni's face began to soften. He asked, "Did someone attack Imani? Has anyone called the police?"

The doctor still wouldn't give Jaloni any information. Jaloni told him, "Imani's my Fiancée and I have the right to know."

The doctor wouldn't budge and told him that he couldn't break patient confidentiality.

Jaloni didn't like the way the doctor was accusing him of beating her. The doctor didn't come out and say it but he knew that is the direction his questions were leading. Jaloni stood there in disbelief. He couldn't believe anyone would accuse him of beating Imani.

"Did she tell you I hit her? I assure you I never laid a hand on her and I never will. Naw, I know she didn't tell you that. You are trying to make it out to be something it's not." Jaloni stated confidently.

Jaloni was still mad but calmer than before. Jaloni attempted to go back into the room and question Imani. The doctor once again told him to let Imani rest and possibly he could come back another day to see her. Jaloni looked at the doctor in shock and left the area. He thought to himself that he would not be back to see Imani, for all he knows there would be police there waiting to arrest him. He stayed cool because he knew he didn't do anything.

CHAPTER 15

Destiny called me, trying to explain her side of the incident. I really didn't want to hear it because I am worried about Imani.

"I told you not to say anything to Imani." I explained.

"She attacks me and I get blamed? How are you going to take her side?" Destiny screeched. "You know what? I don't need this from you. I thought we were friends. You've known me much longer than her and you know I didn't do or say anything to make Imani attack me like that. Like she said, she's been waiting to do that for a long time. You ever wonder why? Your friend is crazy! That's why!"

"Destiny, Imani told me what you said to her. Frankly, I don't have time for this right now. Imani is in the hospital and I am going to see her." I answered.

I wasn't trying to sound cruel but I think it may have come off that way.

"Why is she in the hospital? What happened to her? It couldn't have been me. I barely got a hit in." Destiny asked.

She sounded genuinely worried.

"I don't have all the answers but I will let you know when I know." I answered.

I do know why Imani is in the hospital but I didn't know if she wanted me to tell anyone. Imani is a stickler for secrecy. What Destiny said made me think. Why did Imani want to fight Destiny? I heard Imani say it but thought it was something she said in the heat of the moment. I'm sick of the whole situation and I am not asking anymore questions about it.

I began thinking about what Destiny said to Imani. I decided to ask Destiny about it.

"Destiny, do you only hang out with Imani because I bring her around?"

Destiny was quiet for a long time and she finally answered. "No I like Imani but Jaloni and everyone are right. Denise you know they are. She is too loud and too crude."

"I don't believe they are right. She may need to tone it down at times but all in all she handles herself well." I answered Destiny the way I have always answered when someone asked me about Imani's behavior.

"So you mean to tell me that you have never been embarrassed by the things she does and says? I know you can't say that because I have seen your face and I know you." Destiny asked.

She actually sounded like she is pleading for me to agree with her.

I didn't answer Destiny. I changed the subject and asked Destiny about Helena. Destiny proclaimed that she wasn't seeing Helena anymore. She asked me if I remembered her telling me that before. I remembered but I know I have had changes of heart about someone so why couldn't she. I was thinking it but I didn't say it to her.

Destiny started telling me about Stephon and how they met Saturday in the club. I was so tempted to ask what happened in the bathroom but figured it is too much information. My mind must have wandered because Destiny was asking me if I heard her.

"I'm in love I said." She repeated.

I had to ask, "With who?"

She laughed and said, "Stephon silly. I just told you about him. Are you listening to me at all?"

I was relieved and scared. I heard her alright but I couldn't believe that she was saying it.

"You just met him on Saturday and you are saying that you are in love with him?" I asked Destiny, trying to figure it out in my mind.

"Yeah Denise I am in love with him. I can't explain it; it's just how I feel." Destiny answered.

She sounded a little defensive but sincere.

"So tell me about him?" I asked Destiny, thinking this is going to be another Helena situation.

She began telling me about Stephon. He is a teacher and from Minnesota. He went to George Washington University in DC. She also told me that he loves teaching because he has the opportunity to be a good influence on children in a time where so many people shy away from being role models.

Destiny said, "We have a lot in common. He is so nice and respectful to me. I have never felt the way Stephon makes me feel, before." I told her, "Don't rush into a relationship," telling her "You see what that got me." She said, "OK" and kept talking.

I thought to myself, she actually knew a lot about him but love is a strong word. She told me they talked for the rest of the night on Saturday and all day Sunday. She told me he was such a gentleman and that they didn't even kiss until he was leaving her house on Sunday night. Maybe I was seeing things on Saturday. She seems genuine and if she is happy, I am happy for her. Her other line beeped, she informed me that it is Stephon and she would call me later or tomorrow to see how Imani is doing.

I picked Imani up from the hospital the next day. She asked me to come because she tried calling Jaloni but he was nowhere to be found. I was shocked to see all the flowers that Imani had in her room.

"Who did you make friends with while you were in here? Are they from Jaloni?" I asked Imani while my eyes dotted around the room.

Imani replied, "No! They are not from Jaloni. All I got from him is problems and accusations. They are from Paul. Remember the guy I introduced you to the first time we went to The Twist? The one I work with?"

Imani continued by telling me that he is also who sent the other flowers. That information made me let out a sigh of relief. I was truly glad that mystery was over.

I looked at Imani, she looked sad and tired. I asked if she was OK and she perked up and said, "Yeah. Why do you ask? I am glad to be sprung from this joint. One more thing, though. Can you help me bring these flowers out to the nurse's station?"

"Why are you bringing the flowers to the nurse's station?" I asked Imani.

"I can't bring them home because it is too many of them and also because I do not want to hear Jaloni's mouth. He would have something to say every time he saw the flowers." She answered.

She actually began laughing out loud at the thought of him walking by all of those flowers cursing. I know this because she told me that and asked me to imagine it with her.

"Oh yeah. I see your point." I said laughing with her. I thought to myself that Jaloni is definitely something. I also thought he should be the one here picking her up but I left it alone.

Imani let out a loud sigh before we picked up her bags and headed out of the room. I asked her again if she felt OK and she nodded yes. On that note I left it alone. On the way home Imani asked me what I did on Sunday and I told her that I didn't do much. She laughed and called me boring. That was pretty much the conversation for the ride home.

Upon arriving at Imani's house Imani spotted Jaloni's truck out front. This upset her a little because she tried to call him and he didn't answer the phone. I actually thought I saw him peek out the window when we first pulled up but when I helped Imani in the house with her bags Jaloni was nowhere to be seen. Imani even called out to him but he didn't answer.

Imani gave me a hug and thanked me for picking her up. She alerted me that she is serious about what she asked of me in the hospital and would let me know about developments. I almost forgot what she was talking about until she put her finger over her mouth. Imani hugged me again and told me to apologize to Destiny for her.

Soon as I left, Imani yelled Jaloni's name. She asked him if he could come down and help her bring her bags upstairs. Jaloni didn't answer Imani but came down the stairs after about five minutes. By the time he came down Imani had put the bags in the hall closet and was lying down on the couch. She was watching TV but turned down the volume when Jaloni appeared.

"Hello Jaloni. Didn't you hear me calling you earlier?" Imani asked sarcastically. Imani knew that if Jaloni was in the house he could hear her calling him.

Jaloni just looked at her for a moment. Then he asked, "Where are the bags you want put upstairs?"

"They are in the hall closet. I put them there because I thought you were not here when you didn't answer." She said, staring right back at Jaloni. Imani continued by saying, "I wouldn't have wanted you to come in the house and trip over them."

Jaloni still said nothing directly to her. He took the bags out of the closet and put them upstairs in the bedroom closet. When Jaloni came back downstairs he brought a blanket for Imani to wrap around herself on the couch. When he reached the couch he tossed the blanket over her and kept going toward the kitchen.

Imani just watched him go. She didn't want to say anything to him because she did not want to hear his mouth. Jaloni yelled from the kitchen. "Would you like something to eat or drink while I am in here?"

"No thank you. I am fine right now. I just need rest." Imani replied.

She hoped this meant that he wasn't going to start in on her.

"OK. Let me know if you change your mind." Jaloni said. He almost sounded like he meant it. "Where are your flowers?" He asked.

"I left the flowers at the hospital. I didn't think it would be appropriate to bring them home. Plus they can be given to someone else."

Imani answered just knowing Jaloni was going to start.

"OK but you could have kept them if you wanted to. I know you love flowers even though you act like you don't." Jaloni told her.

Imani raised her eyebrow and rose up on the couch. She patiently waited for the other shoe to fall. It didn't though. All of a sudden she heard the back door open and close and Jaloni was gone. He left the house but she couldn't tell if he left the property or not. All she did know is that is the last she heard from him for a long time. She didn't see him again until she was getting ready for bed.

Jaloni was in awe when Imani changed to go to bed. He saw the black and blue bruises on her back and arm and was saddened. He didn't say anything because she didn't say anything.

Jaloni really wanted to know where those bruises came from because he knew for damn sure they didn't come from him.

He turned away from Imani because he didn't want her to notice him staring at the bruises. He figured she would tell him what happened in her own time. He wondered how someone could hurt her like that and why she didn't tell him who it is so he could beat their ass.

Jaloni was very scared. Imani didn't even face him in bed. She didn't kiss him good night or anything. He wondered if she was raped but didn't know how to bring it up. He just thought to himself that she is definitely not acting like herself. He also wondered if she is mad at him and why. He tried to be there for her and she appeared to turn him away at every turn.

Jaloni thought about reaching out to hold Imani but changed his mind when he thought about it again. He didn't want to hurt her mentally or physically and he had no idea how much pain she is actually in. Jaloni laid there for a while then turned to see if Imani was sleeping.

When it appeared that she was asleep, Jaloni looked at her more closely. He noticed earlier that she was walking kind of funny and now she is holding her stomach while she slept. He was so worried about Imani that he couldn't sleep at all. He just played with Imani's hair while she slept.

CHAPTER 16

Imani was happy in her new home. It was a loft style apartment with an elevated area for her bedroom. The apartment also had its own elevator entrance. It is glamorous and Imani remembered how she used to dream about living in an apartment like this. She always liked the way they looked in the movies so when the Realtor told her she had one in the South End section of Boston Imani jumped on it.

Imani thought that the rent is a little steep but it is in the range she could afford. The Realtor laughed at Imani because she began making faces when she found out how much the rent is going to be. She didn't think about how much it would be with the deposit and first and last months' rent payments. She felt comfortable paying it though because she saved a lot of money while living with Jaloni.

She felt bad about leaving while Jaloni is out of town but she didn't want the drama of doing it while he was there. She knows he would have tried to stop her and she is determined to move on with her life. She also knew he would make a scene. Actually she didn't know how Jaloni would have responded because he has been all over the place in the last few months.

Imani thought about the fact that Jaloni only came to see her once in the hospital and that they had barely spoken since she came home from the hospital. She knew it is time. Jaloni went on a trip with the team that he didn't have to go on. Usually she would be mad about it but this time she was happy for the opportunity to make her move. Paul and I came over and helped her move her stuff out.

Paul has really turned out to be a good friend to Imani. Imani said she still sees him looking at her like he wants more than a friendship. She called him on it once and he said he can't help it, she is so beautiful. He told Imani that is equal to being outside on a clear night and not looking at the stars. He also assured her that he understood that she is his friend. Paul also let Imani know that he cherishes her friendship and wouldn't do anything to lose it.

Two weeks after Imani moved in, I came to her apartment bearing housewarming gifts. She opened the door with a big grin on her face. It is so good to see her smiling again.

"What? No liquor heifer?" Imani called out.

All I could do is smile because that was music to my ears. She is starting to be her old self again.

"You mean to tell me you've been living here for two weeks and you haven't bought any liquor yet? You should be ashamed of yourself." I hollered back.

We both laughed at that.

"If you're staying we can order food. I didn't cook anything." She said. "You're staying. What do you want to eat?"

I told her Chinese.

She said, "Good because I am already on the phone with the Chinese restaurant." She laughed out loud; it is so good to hear her laughing.

I asked Imani how she is doing and she responded, "Better than I have been in a long time." She definitely looked it. I began smiling at her. When she saw me smiling she smiled back and said, "What are you looking at?"

"Look at you being all independent." I answered.

We both laughed at that but I really couldn't remember a time when Imani didn't have a man in her life. I know she has never lived on her own before except for the college dorms and that doesn't count because she still had roommates. She moved right out of her parent's house into Jaloni's house.

Imani gave me a grand tour of her apartment. She had fixed it up nice. She had a king-size bed in the middle of the apartment. The bed was a four-poster canopy bed surrounded by silk curtains. She had the place decorated with candles all around. They smelled and looked good.

We sat in Imani's kitchen when the Chinese food arrived. She had the kitchen decorated in all dark brown wood and the appliances were black. I complimented her on her apartment and she responded that I should have known she would hook it up because of her good taste. I couldn't help but laugh at that. Imani was definitely the person I remember her being before everything began unraveling with Jaloni.

I stayed at Imani's house for a long time. We talked about everything except Jaloni. She apologized for fixing me up with Tyrone and acting like it was my fault when Jaloni yelled at her about it. She explained that Jaloni didn't know he was married either and because Tyrone was so young he didn't think to ask him.

We also talked about old times, college and how we used to hang out. Imani thought about it and said.

"The real world really has a way of fucking things up. We don't hang like we did in college."

"Yeah but if we didn't work we wouldn't be able to live so what you going to do?" I answered.

"See I wish we didn't have to work. I kind of hoped things worked out with Jaloni and Tyrone so we could have the security and time to hang out. We could go shopping and chill by the pool or something. But there is no need of talking about that now because they are gone." She said.

I think Imani meant for that to sound sad but the relief in her voice overpowered the sadness of the comment. We raised our glasses of juice and toasted to the future and to one day being able to not work.

Jaloni came home and he realized something was wrong right away. He screamed out to Imani but got no answer. He ran upstairs and noticed a lot of things missing. At first he thought the house was robbed but as he looked around he noticed none of his things were missing. He went into the bedroom and looked in the closet. Imani's side was all cleared out.

Jaloni fell to the floor in the closet, put his hands over his face, holding back the tears. He isn't going to cry. He is going to find her and bring her back. He needed her. He thought in his mind they were going through some things but it couldn't be over. It wouldn't be over.

Then Jaloni's pride kicked in. "Damn her!" he screamed. She is only doing this to make me marry her or something he thought. It's not going to work. He tried to call her on her cell phone to tell her exactly what he thought of her plan but the number was disconnected. When he walked in the kitchen her cell phone was laying on the table. Jaloni didn't want to play into her hands but he is beginning to worry.

Jaloni called my number but there was no answer. He thought about leaving a message, figuring she had to be staying with me for protection if nothing else but thought against it. He slammed down the phone when he heard the answering machine. From the number of calls on my answering machine, Jaloni did that more than once.

He called around to some of the connections he had in the city to see if anyone has seen her. No one had. Impossible! Imani doesn't go that long without going out for attention he thought.

He knew her and she had to show up at a club, restaurant or somewhere. He would call her at work tomorrow and talk to her.

He looked around again and realized how much stuff she took and got even more scared. He got in his car and drove to my house but no one was home. He banged on the door for a long time but no one answered but a neighbor telling him to keep it down. He sat out front for a couple of hours and then called it a night. "Yeah," he thought. "I will call her at work tomorrow."

Jaloni called Imani's office at 9:06 am. He didn't get any sleep but he was wide-awake. When he got Imani's voicemail he thought that she had to be there. Imani was never late for work. He contemplated leaving a message but thought it would be best to speak to her in person. What Jaloni really wanted to do was go get her and make her come back home with him. He didn't understand why she left. He thought about all of the things that they have been through and then slammed the phone down.

"Why do I want her back?" He thought, thinking about the time he found out that she cheated on him and all the times that people told him that she was out with other men.

Maybe he is the sucker they all called him. He didn't care what others had to say. He thought about leaving her before but couldn't.

This is scaring him so much because he loves her so much. He figured that he would give her time to think. He knew that she'd never find anyone that is going to treat her like him or put up with her shit like he does.

Imani knew Jaloni was home when she listened to her voicemail. She heard the phone slam down but no words. She knew it was Jaloni but she isn't going to call him. She is going to stay strong. She really didn't mean to hurt Jaloni but questioned if he had the same consideration for her. He really stressed her out over the past few months and she didn't know if their relationship is worth saving. She doubted it.

Paul came over to Imani's desk and startled her. He came to ask if Imani had plans for lunch.

She was out of it and it took her a while to figure out what Paul wanted. When she figured it out she answered, "No. Why?"

He told her that a new restaurant opened around the corner and he wanted to check it out.

He jokingly added, "Don't worry it is not a date."

Imani said, "I know it's not a date, friend." They both laughed.

Paul told Imani he would see her at 12:30 and walked off, wondering how long he could continue just being Imani's friend. He turned back a couple of times and waved at Imani. This made her giggle. He turned back one more time to look at her before he went into his office. Damn! She is beautiful he thought as he sat down at his desk and attempted to get some work done.

Imani called me and we talked for a while, both trying to avoid the obvious topic. Imani broke first. "Jaloni is back in town."

"I know. My neighbor told me that someone fitting his description was banging on my door last night. She asked me is he is my boyfriend and told me he was rude." I answered. "She said he was out there for over an hour banging and screaming and when she told him to keep it down he told her to go to hell."

"I don't want to talk to him, Denise. I am not ready for that yet. I am having the tech people in the office change my extension and the receptionist has strict orders not to give the new one out to anyone." I told her, "Take your time and don't worry about him. Your main concern should be you. You've been through a lot in the past few months. You'll talk when you are ready."

Imani perked up all of a sudden and asked me if I wanted to go to lunch with her and Paul. I said yes and we planned to meet at 12:30 outside her building. She told me she loved me and said goodbye. I returned her sentiment and we hung up.

I reached Imani's office building at 12:30 but there was no sight of Imani or Paul. I looked around to see if they possibly went to the stores across the street or began walking to the restaurant. I didn't see them but I did see Jaloni sitting in his black BMW truck.

He saw me too and decided to leave. Jaloni sped off, down the street, making pedestrians scatter. He stopped for the red light and I could see him stick his head out of the window and look back. The light changed to green and he took off, speeding again, down the street. A few minutes later, Paul and Imani came out of the building. They were both smiling and laughing so I decided against telling Imani that Jaloni was just here.

At lunch we sat in a booth that faced the street. I kept looking out the window, watching the people and thinking. I also looked to see if Jaloni would come back. I heard Imani giggling but paid it no mind. Paul and Imani are always like that when they are together. Then what I thought was the waiter asked me if I had been served. I turned to answer him and saw it was Darrell. When I turned around I noticed there was a woman with him. I shot Darrell a confused look but played it off by asking, "What another job? Leave some jobs for other people."

Everyone laughed hard at that, including the woman with Darrell.

"I am not really your waiter silly. I just want to know if you are being served." He said with a wink.

"No really I just stopped by to say hi and see how you lovely ladies are doing." He continued, still laughing at my joke.

He reminded us that we could stop by the club any time on him. After he finished talking, he and the lady left.

"Eww! You are still always messing with the help." Imani laughed.

I responded by telling her, "Darrell owns The Twist. Didn't I tell you that before? So technically he is not help."

I guess not because Imani was awed. I thought I had told Imani but with all the things going on it must have slipped her mind or mine.

I went back to looking out the window, wondering why Darrell made an effort to come over and talk to me. He had a woman with him. I just thought to myself that men are unbelievable. They always want their cake and eat it too. I also thought that woman couldn't have been so smart either to allow him to come up to me the way he did. I continued thinking about the episode when the real waiter interrupted me.

CHAPTER 17

Destiny and Stephon have been going out for a while now. They are spending so much time together; Destiny barely has any time for anything or anyone else but she didn't mind. She likes being with Stephon and still feels the same way about him she did on day one. They decided to go to The Twist on Saturday just to do something different. They usually hung out at Destiny's house or went to the movies or dinner.

Destiny was hoping to see me there because she hasn't spoken to me since our last phone call and argument about Imani. Equally, she hoped that Imani did not show up but she knew if I was coming that Imani is most likely coming with me. Destiny hasn't spoken to her either. She hadn't even spoken about that night again, not even to Stephon.

Inside the club, Destiny and Stephon got some drinks at the bar and then walked around for a while. They stopped when he found some of his friends that he plays basketball with on the weekends. Well that he used to play with until he met Destiny. They were all joking with him about that.

Destiny spotted Helena over in the corner of the room with some football players from the Patriots. Destiny hoped that Helena didn't see her but she did. When Helena saw Destiny, she ran up and gave her a hug. Then Helena tried to kiss Destiny on the lips.

Destiny jumped back and put her hand over Helena's face. Helena got really angry and reached out to slap Destiny in the face. Lucky for Destiny, she hadn't put her hand down. She barely had the chance to block Helena's slap.

Stephon's boys started ooohhhing so he looked to see what is going on. He said, "Damn," then jumped between Destiny and

Helena. Stephon looked and realized that Helena wasn't Imani so he asked what was going on. "My bitch and I have some unfinished business." Helena said, laughing.

Stephon was confused.

"Oh! She didn't tell you about me? How I am the best she ever had in bed and how she has never had the feelings she had during sex with me, with a man?" Helena continued, smiling a demonic-like grin, and staring at Stephon like she is measuring him up.

Destiny just stood there. She couldn't say anything and had nowhere to run. Destiny began looking around, trying to find a way out of this situation when Helena reached out to slap her again. Destiny closed her eyes and blocked her face. She opened her eyes just in time to see Imani grab Helena's arm. Everyone looked shocked.

Imani asked, "Who is this heifer?"

Imani held Helena by the arm. Nobody said a word so Imani twisted Helena around to see her face and asked, "Who are you?"

She told Imani, "I am Destiny's girlfriend."

Helena had an evil smirk on her face and was very pleased with herself because of the look on Imani's face. Imani could have shitted her pants. Her expression was truly priceless.

Imani looked at Destiny. She began smiling, thinking she will never let Destiny live this one down. Imani remembered that she had Helena by the arm when she heard her squeal. She looked down at Helena, twisted her arm harder, and told her she would let her go if she keeps her hands to herself. Helena promised and Imani let her go with a push. Helena walked off mumbling about it not being over.

We could hear Helena telling the people with her, she had to smack her hoe up. They were all laughing as Helena went into graphic details about her and Destiny. She was playing to a full house and had the attention of all of them. We could hear them ooohing and laughing from where we were standing.

Imani and Stephon were looking at Destiny like she had two heads. Imani then did something that totally shocked everyone. She walked over to Destiny and hugged her. Destiny looked scared, like she didn't trust Imani. For a minute I didn't either. Imani told Destiny she is sorry for before and that she loved her.

Imani held Destiny for what seemed like forever then pulled her away and began looking at her like she had never seen her before. Imani looked around and noticed Stephon still watching.

She annoyingly asked, "Who is he?"

Imani thought he was just a nosy bystander or with Helena.

Destiny said, "He was my boyfriend."

Destiny sadly looked toward the ground. She didn't know how else to answer that question.

"Was your boyfriend? What? You're going back to that chick? What do you mean was?" Stephon inquired.

"I don't know. I didn't think..." Destiny said.

Imani and I were both hugging Destiny, holding her up. She was wobbly and looked like she wanted to disappear more than anything. I think we all wanted to know the answer to Stephon's question. I remembered Destiny saying Helena had some kind of pull on her and wondered if this episode triggered something within Destiny. I was looking at her mostly to see if she was OK but also to see if she is going to answer Stephon's question. She told me she loved Stephon and I am hoping she doesn't let Helena ruin it.

Destiny snapped out of it. She saw everyone looking at her

so she grabbed Stephon by the arm and hurried him out of the club. They didn't even stop to get their coats, which Stephon reminded her of when they got outside. He was freezing but Destiny couldn't feel a thing. She didn't stop so he didn't stop either.

They got in the car and went to her apartment. Destiny didn't speak the whole ride home and Stephon didn't pressure her. Soon as they got in the door Destiny started undressing Stephon. She got his shirt off and started kissing him intensely. He had mixed emotions about this. He wanted Destiny so bad but they really needed to talk about what happened tonight. He snapped out of his daze when he heard his pants hit the floor.

He backed up and asked, "Why are you doing this?"

Destiny just looked at Stephon in a seductive way.

He almost forgot why he stopped her. "We need to talk about tonight."

Destiny started kissing Stephon again and didn't stop until she noticed he wasn't responding. She walked away, through her bedroom and into the bathroom. Stephon heard the door lock but didn't think anything of it until about an hour passed.

Destiny wasn't doing anything in the bathroom. She didn't want to face Stephon. He knocked on the bathroom door and she ignored him. She was embarrassed, more so about what happened here than what happened in the club. She felt like she had something to prove to Stephon and to herself. She wanted him and often wondered why they haven't had sex but didn't want to sound sluttish by asking him.

"Destiny, come out because I'm not leaving." He yelled.

The phone rang and Stephon let it ring. It kept ringing so Stephon finally answered it. He shouted hello into the receiver and was barraged by Helena.

"Is my bitch there?" Helena asked laughing.

"She's busy. Can you call her back some other time, like never?"

Stephon said and hung up the phone.

Helena called right back and began telling Stephon things about their relationship. Stephon listened in awe but couldn't say anything or hang up. She told him about the threesomes and about their sex life. Helena finished by telling Stephon, "She will always be mine! Men don't turn her on like women do. She's probably faking with you." Helena laughed one more time and hung up the phone in Stephon's ear.

Stephon thought about it and decided it would be best if he left. He quietly picked up his clothes and belongings and walked out the front door, blowing a kiss at Destiny as he closed the door. Helena's statements rung in his head like a bell. He wondered if Helena is right. He loved Destiny and the thought of her faking it with him is hard to take.

Stephon got home and immediately checked his messages. There were none. He hoped Destiny had come out the bathroom and called him. He got undressed and laid down on the bed. He looked at the phone every few minutes, as if trying to will it into ringing but it didn't. Somewhere in between looks, he fell asleep.

Destiny finally came out of the bathroom. She called out to Stephon but got no answer. She walked through her apartment and realized that Stephon was gone. Destiny thought about calling him but then decided against it. She isn't ready to face him anyway. She played everything that happened back in her mind and wondered why this is happening to her.

She thought that Stephon must think she is crazy or a hoe.

He probably will not want to be with her because of the drama she has in her life. Destiny laid down on the bed and thought that she couldn't even imagine what Stephon must think of her for being with Helena. Destiny decided to give Stephon time to take it all in before she calls him.

Destiny decided she not to cry. She didn't feel like her relationship with Stephon is over. She knew he loves her and she loves him so it can all be worked out. Time is all that is needed. She felt so sorry that he had to experience that and wondered what he is thinking. She really wanted to call him and explain but she didn't have all of the answers.

She also thought about calling Helena and cursing her out. Destiny wondered how Helena could do that to her and why. She didn't do anything to her. After thinking about it a little longer she decided she didn't want to hear Helena's excuses. She knew that is all she would have got from Helena. Excuses.

CHAPTER 18

Jaloni couldn't take it anymore. It had been weeks since he returned to Boston and he had not heard from Imani. She didn't return the phone messages he left for her at her job and the number he had no longer connected him directly to Imani. He calls my house frequently but hangs up because he has nothing to say to me. In his mind, I am the reason Imani left him.

Jaloni began thinking about it. He knows how girls get together and knock the man of the friend that is in a relationship. Telling her, "He is cheating or he isn't treating you right, girl. I would leave him." That is their favorite line Jaloni thought. The more he thought about it, the madder he got. Calm down Jaloni. It's all good he thought while trying to figure out what to do next. He thought about flowers but figured that would only make her mad. He remembered how she reacted when that poor sap at her job began sending her flowers.

Before Jaloni knew what he was doing, he was at my door. He banged for about a half-hour before I walked up behind him.

"She's not here." I said. "She got an apartment and says she doesn't want to see you."

"Thanks to you. I know you've been poisoning her mind against me because you can't keep a man." Jaloni responded angrily.

My first instinct was to curse this asshole out. Let him know about himself. Lucky for him I realize he is in pain or whatever it is that men feel when they mess up and lose a woman. I just looked at him like he is crazy, walking right past him.

"Why?" Jaloni screamed and snapped me out of my thought. "I know you have to know I love her to put up with all her shit."

I looked at him and saw that he was definitely in pain.

"That woman cheated on me constantly and I never said a thing. I know about all of them. I let everyone call me a punk and tell me I should leave her."

He was on the verge of crying but he is not innocent so I had no sympathy for him.

"What about your cheating, Jaloni? What about you talking down to her, calling her a whore and always accusing her of things?"

"OOOHH!!! Is that what she has been telling you? She was always accusing me of doing things and cheating. I have never cheated on her. At least I was accusing her of things she actually did."

He continued yelling and I know my neighbors were listening so I told him to come in the house.

"So you never cheated?" I asked as I opened the door.

"Never! He repeated.

He sounded so sincere.

"Never?" I asked again.

This time he just stared at me, totally frustrated with my line of questioning.

When I opened the door he went straight to the couch and sat down before I invited him to sit and put his hands in his head.

"God as my witness, on my father's grave I have never cheated on her. I'm sorry about calling her names but I got frustrated with her behavior. She would go out, people would come to me talking about what she had on, who she was all hugged up with, left with, everything you don't want to hear about the woman you want to spend the rest of your life with."

He kept going, telling me how he tried to rationalize the position she put him in. He told me that her continuing to act that way was a smack in the face in his eyes.

"If anything she doesn't love me. That's what you should have been telling her. Not the other way around." He was almost crying.

I didn't know how to react to what I just heard. I shook my head.

"I can't give you her phone number, address, or anything. I wish I could help you but I can't."

"What happened to her?" he asked.

I didn't know what he meant but he continued,

"When she was in the hospital..." Jaloni began, "Why was she in the hospital? She said something about stress but the doctors wouldn't talk to me. Why couldn't she tell me what happened to her? Did I do it? Is that why she moved out? I never laid a hand on her. They kept talking to me like I hit her."

I told Jaloni to calm down and explained that the bruises came from her fighting with Destiny.

"Fighting with Destiny?" Jaloni asked. "I thought you are friends with Destiny?"

"We are friends with Destiny. Sometimes friends disagree and they took it too far." I answered.

Jaloni just shook his head.

"Y'all are too much. I'll never understand women's relationships." He was laughing now. "Tell your girl I'm sorry and I love her. That is if you're still talking to her by the time you see her."

Apparently someone said something funny. He may have been laughing out of relief, knowing now nobody could accuse him of beating Imani.

Jaloni and I continued to talk. He apologized to me for the whole Tyrone thing. Those were his exact words. He told me he is definitely out of the matchmaking business and realized I was telling the truth when Tyrone showed up this year with his wife and children in tow. He told me I am not so bad. He said he guess he needed someone to blame for Imani's behavior, other than himself or her.

Jaloni was still laughing as he walked out my apartment. I gained a lot of respect for Jaloni after we talked. He had gone through it with Imani and suffered for a long time. I wondered if I should tell Imani Jaloni stopped by or what he said to me. I thought back to him saying I sabotaged their relationship because I could not keep a man. I never once gave Imani advice or told her to leave Jaloni. I should have let him know that.

"What am I saying?" I thought. I can keep a man if he is a good man. I just haven't met a man worth keeping. Then I thought about my own relationships. I wondered if I have sabotaged any of them. I also wondered if that is what Imani were doing all those times she cheated, sabotaging her and Jaloni's relationship. I felt a little bad for him now that I have heard his side of the story.

I thought of calling Imani and asking her about her relationship and why she thought Jaloni was cheating on her. I know men lie but I could see it in Jaloni's eyes that he is telling the truth. I guess she just got caught up in the Player myths. How NBA players have a woman, or man, in every city they play in. It is hard to trust someone that is away a lot.

While thinking I must have dozed off because I was awaken by the phone. I answered the phone frustrated and the voice on the other end said, "I am using my friend calling card but I see that friendly is not home."

Still dazed I replied, "Huh"

The person began laughing and I caught on that it was Darrell.

"What do you want Darrell?" my mind went directly back to him being with the woman in the restaurant.

"I told you a friend." He shot back.

"Where's your friend from the restaurant?" I asked. "She thought you were pretty funny."

He explained that she is his attorney and that he doesn't mix business with pleasure ever.

"Especially not with women." He answered laughing. "They'll get you every time."

He asked how I have been and about Tyrone. He told me I didn't have to answer if it is too personal but I explained to him, "I broke one of my rules."

He asked what rule and I answered, "My not dating athletes rule."

He said, "You are going to punish all athletes for the stupidity of a few? That's just wrong."

I asked him, "Why do you care about my decision? It's just like you're not mixing business with pleasure rule."

Darrell told me, "I am a former football player. I quit because I was traded 4 times in 2 years and got sick of it. When the Patriots were planning to trade me, I asked if there was another way out of my contract. They said no and told me they would sue me if I didn't comply." He got an attorney, the one I saw him with that day, which advised him to retire after hearing him talk.

He told me, "I was worried about money and living but my attorney assured me everything would be OK. She assembled a team of financial advisors who mapped out a plan that would provide for me for the rest of my life and most of my children's lives."

"So how many children do you have?" I asked trying to make it sound like I was joking.

"A typical woman. I just poured out my heart and all you heard is children. I don't have any children yet."

He laughed but I could tell the question agitated him. I apologized and asked him about bouncing at the clubs. He answered. "It is another one of my business ventures. My buddy was approached to be a bodyguard and realized more and more athletes and entertainers were using bodyguards. He approached me about the venture and we went in as partners."

"Why were you working on New Year's Eve?" I asked.

"To meet you." He answered quickly. "No, I was working because the place is so big and only a few of us can carry guns. I also wanted to check the place out for ideas for my club."

We talked for what seemed like hours. I laughed a lot and I liked that. I especially liked getting to know the real him instead of the pretender I met on New Year's Eve. We ended the conversation with plans to go to dinner and to Atlanta in the fall.

I got off the phone and thought what I am thinking. I don't know this man. I am not ready to get into another relationship, especially with another athlete. I will tell him that the next time he calls. Better yet, I should call him back right now and tell him. I thought about it some more and decided against calling but I would definitely tell him.

———————————

Jaloni smiled all the way home. He left my place with a new understanding of who I am as well as a couple of answers about Imani. He is still baffled at the hospital thing, why everyone acted like there is a big secret that was all that happened. The smile then left Jaloni's face. He figured that there had to be more. Why were they acting like he abused her if they knew that she had a fight with Destiny?

Jaloni began to wonder if Imani told them he hit her. He heard of women who did things like that but can't believe Imani is one of them. If this is the case why hasn't she used it yet? His mind wandered. What could Imani want that he hasn't already given her and how could abuse allegations get it. Jaloni got really frightened. He thought about coming back to my place, asking me what Imani wanted and why she made the doctors believe that he abused her.

After he thought it through a little more he decided to let it go. There is nothing Imani could do to him or get from him. He had the Ace anyway. He knew she got the bruises from fighting with Destiny. He also had proof that Imani was unfaithful to him in the past. That should be enough to keep her away if it came to that.

Jaloni hoped it never came to that because he still loves her and wants to be with her. He banged on his steering wheel in frustration. "Dang! Why can't this be easier? All I want is to love this woman. Why is it so hard?" Jaloni yelled out loud.

He realized how loud he was yelling when the person in the car next him began staring at him. He shook his head and thought, all he needed is for that person to be some nosy person who is going to tell the media that he was in his car talking to himself and acting crazy. He started laughing just thinking about the gossip column in the local paper. Oh well, he thought, let them think I am crazy. He was still laughing as he sped away from the light.

CHAPTER 19

Destiny felt bad. She didn't understand what happened to her and she had no idea how to fix it. She loves Stephon. She felt that from the moment she met him. She figured he wouldn't ever speak to her again so she still hasn't attempted to call him.

Destiny is so mad at Helena and didn't understand how she could do that. Destiny began thinking it is her fault also for not telling Stephon about her past. The phone rang, it is Helena. Destiny is about to get her answers.

Destiny answered the phone and Helena started by saying.

"Destiny don't hang up on me. I'm sorry. I don't know what came over me." She continued, "OK, yes I do. I got jealous. I know we said we were going to keep our relationship a friendship but I love you. I saw you with him and the happiness in your eyes and I flipped out."

Destiny exclaimed, "You should have talked to me about your feelings. At least then I would have an idea of where we stood."

"Would you be with me if I did? You made it perfectly clear that you are not a lesbian." Helena responded.

Destiny didn't have an answer to her question and she let Helena know. There was a long silence on the phone then Helena spoke, "Well I just wanted to tell you I am sorry and let you know how I feel. I won't bother you anymore. I'll leave the decision in your hands. Goodbye."

Destiny was so confused. What decision was Helena talking

about? She knew at that moment that she had to call Stephon. Maybe he thought she was making a decision also. She picked up the phone, dialed the number and hung it up before anyone answered. She repeated this ritual about three more times before her phone rang. Destiny whispered hello into the receiver.

"Destiny?" the voice on the other end asked. "What is wrong? Are you OK?"

"Stephon?" Destiny asked.

She was shocked that he called her back. She thought to herself that she must have forgot to block her number the last time she called.

He answered yes and that he is happy she called.

"I thought you didn't want to talk to me anymore. Why did you hang up though?" Stephon questioned Destiny.

"Why would you think that?" Destiny asked. "You didn't do anything. I did. I didn't know what to say to you. I thought you would think I am a terrible person. I wanted to talk to you but thought against it as I dialed the phone."

Stephon told her, "I could never think you are a terrible person. I love you and will support you no matter what your decision is."

Destiny told him, "I love you and I want to be with you and only you."

Stephon didn't know what to think about Destiny's declaration after they finished talking. What made her call after not calling for so long? He does love her but still couldn't shake the thought of all the things Helena told him about Destiny, most of all what Helena told him about women turning her on more than men. He thought about it constantly since Helena said it to him.

Stephon wondered if it would ever be only him. He had so many other questions in his head. There are so many things they would have to work out before he could even think about being with Destiny. Stephon is looking for so much more than a girlfriend at this point in his life and had to know if her feelings for women will affect their relationship.

Stephon decided to get in his car and go talk to Destiny. He needed to know if it could be worked out. Destiny was shocked when she opened her door and Stephon was standing there. She didn't know whether to hug him or close the door. She decided that she would follow his lead.

Stephon reached out for Destiny and to his surprise she embraced him so tight he thought she would never let go. He's happy but apprehensive about her welcoming him this way.

Destiny spoke first. "Hey, what are you doing here? I'm not upset about it but I didn't expect to see you."

"I had to see you in person. I know we discussed this on the phone but I still have questions." Stephon said.

"OK. Questions like what?" Destiny asked.

She suspected she isn't going to like where this conversation is headed.

She managed to curb her desire to roll her eyes and dismiss Stephon. She invited him in and offered him something to drink or eat. Stephon declined her offers. He sat on the couch looking serious. He looked so serious that Destiny began to worry.

"You said you wanted to talk?" Destiny asked apprehensively.

She really didn't want to talk.

"Yes. I want to talk about us. Where do you see us going?" Stephon asked, dodging the question he really wanted answered.

"I don't know where we are going but I hope we are going far. I like you a lot, more than a lot." Destiny sounded like she is pleading with Stephon.

Stephon just looked at Destiny. She looks sincere, he thought. He really hoped that she isn't lying to him or "faking it" as Helena told him. He attempted to get up the nerve to ask her the question that he really wanted to ask her.

"The night I was at your house the phone rang. It was Helena. She talked to me about your relationship with her." Stephon began but Destiny cut him off.

"I'm not a lesbian. It was a one-time thing. Now I think it is the worst decision I have ever made in my life." Destiny said.

Her words were rushed and this made Stephon really worried.

"She told me that you told her that you will never feel the way you felt with her with a man. Is that true?" Stephon asked.

"That was before I met you. What I told her is that I haven't had an explosive sexual relationship with a man. That is all that I meant when I said that to Helena." Destiny stated.

She was so mad at Helena for this whole mess but she wouldn't give the satisfaction of letting her know her plan worked. She is not going to call Helena.

"So am I going to be enough for you or are you going to need a chick on the side or something?" Stephon asked Destiny.

Stephon regretted it the moment it came out of his mouth.

Destiny looked shocked but she didn't get mad.

She answered him by saying, "No I won't need a chick on the side. Ever! My relationship with you is different. I could tell that from the beginning. You stimulate me in so many ways. I know sex with you is going to very stimulating. I love you."

Stephon wanted to shout. He was so happy at that moment and so glad that Destiny did not throw him out when he asked her that chick on the side question. Damn he knew it from the moment they met. This is his wife. But he didn't want to rush things and didn't feel now is the time to ask her to marry him.

Stephon got up, went over to where Destiny was standing. He stepped closer and closer. All the time expecting Destiny to move or tell him to move but she didn't. He kissed her, she kissed him back. Yeah it is just like he remembered it. They did this for a while before Stephon interrupted. He said that he had to go. He only came over to talk to her.

Destiny stood in shock. Why is he leaving? Oh my God it's over she thought. She couldn't believe that he would do her like this. She told him she loved him. Why did he just up and leave her like that? Destiny wanted to cry but she is sick of crying over men. She is sick of crying period and refused to.

Stephon stayed parked outside of Destiny's house for the longest time. He thought he shouldn't have bolted out of Destiny's house like he did but he had to. He was starting to get aroused and he didn't want Destiny to think that all he wanted was to have sex. He wanted her to know that she meant more than that to him.

Stephon still wanted to think through Destiny's answers and see where her head is at. She said it was a one-time thing but if those feelings are there how can she be sure. He thought back to how she said it is the biggest mistake of her. Damn he hoped it is true because the alternative is Helena's version of the story is the truth.

The whole time Stephon drove he wanted to turn back. He wanted to take Destiny in his arms and make sure everything is going to be alright. He wanted to tell her that he wants to marry her. But he couldn't bring himself to do it. When he looked up he was at home. There is definitely no turning back now. He got out of the car and went in the house.

Stephon was happy to see a message on his voicemail when he got home. He hoped it was from Destiny. If it is erratic or in

Fuck you form he would know he made the right decision. But if she is sweet and confused he would definitely think about answering her call.

The phone call wasn't from Destiny. It was from the University of St. Louis. He wondered what it's about so he listened. The message stated that they received his resume from a headhunter and wanted to talk to him in further detail about his goals and future. They said they would like to speak to him about the possibility of offering him a position as a professor at the University.

Stephon called the university back and scheduled an interview for the following week. He thought that the timing isn't perfect but the opportunity is. He thought it through in his mind and believed that he's doing the right thing. He also thought it would get his mind off Destiny. He figured if she didn't call him by the time he went to St. Louis he would call her when he got back. That way they both would have time to think everything over.

CHAPTER 20

Atlanta is a beautiful city and Darrell made sure I saw all of it and what it had to offer during my weekend visit. He explained to me during one of our outings that Atlanta is always crawling with celebrities. They are everywhere. He gets at least one in his club every weekend. They cause a lot of havoc but it's all good and good for business.

He started the tour when he picked me up from the airport. He got off the highway, saying he wanted to show me the scenic route. He asked if I am tired. I said no because I am so wired I wouldn't have gotten any sleep anyway. I have so much adrenaline rushing. Partly because I am in a city I have never been to before and partly because it is the first time I am seeing Darrell in a long time.

As we drove down Peachtree Street, he showed me a lot of points of interest. There seemed to be something impressive on every block. I tried to equate it with a part of Boston but couldn't think of one with so much diversity. He told me we were in the Buckhead section of Atlanta and if I turned to the left I could see P. Diddy's restaurant, Justin's. I turned and there it was. I got so excited about that and what I have seen of the city so far I didn't even notice when he turned off Peachtree.

"This is the main attraction of Buckhead." Darrell said grinning.

Darrell glowed with pride.

"Oh? Yeah? What is it?" I asked teasing him. I knew exactly what it is because the sign is the same as the one in Boston.

"Yeah, this is the spot. Actually the whole area was the spot until recently when the problems began."

"What type of problems?" I asked.

"The neighborhood is not as safe as it used to be. It's keeping a lot of the people I want to frequent my club away." He said with a sad look on his face. "I might have to find a new location for the club if the police and neighborhood can't find a solution. There were even a couple of murders around here in the past year. It's nothing like it was when I went to the University of Georgia and we used to make weekend trips down here to party."

"You went to the University of Georgia? I didn't know you went there." I inquired.

"You never asked that's why. Did I mention how happy I am that you came to visit or how much I am going to spoil you this weekend?"

His smile was worth a million dollars to me at that moment.

"Really? We'll see how you feel in two days. You'll probably be breaking the speed limit to get me to the airport so you can have your space back." I laughed.

"Naw. I'll only rush you to the airport if you want to go. Personally I wouldn't mind if you stayed forever." He continued smiling. I looked over at him and I could see he is serious. I thought we were going to get out and go inside but he drove off.

He turned back onto Peachtree and continued the tour. He showed me Lenox Mall area before he got back on the highway and headed for his home. He kept turning to look at me as if he thought I was going to disappear or something. The ride on the highway was so smooth that I felt myself drifting to sleep and decided not to fight it.

When I woke up I was on his bed.

"Why didn't you wake me? I could have got up and walked." I asked.

I was also kind of self-conscious, imagining how heavy I must have been to carry.

"It is no problem. I told you I am going to spoil you this weekend. Are you rested?"

"Yeah I feel good."

"Well I laid some towels out for you. A robe and scented bath oils if you want to take a bath before dinner. What do you feel like eating? They have it all in this town." He said.

Darrell was still smiling. I wondered if he would smile like that all weekend. I truly hope so because it's a beautiful smile and I am still in love with those dimples.

I truly believe Atlanta has it all. Celebrities were not the only ones Atlanta was crawling with. The city is crawling with Black people. They are all over the place. I noticed it when we were driving and I am impressed. I had heard that Atlanta is considered the premiere Chocolate Cities but I never imagined that I would see so many just by riding down the street. It is a beautiful sight.

Imani sat in her apartment thinking about Jaloni. She did not want to talk to him but she did miss him. She was confused. How come he isn't doing anything to get her back? How could he just give up on her like that? It's probably best; she didn't need him or his scrutiny.

She decided she would go out this weekend and find someone to replace Jaloni. Yeah, it has been long enough to get over a breakup. Imani isn't over Jaloni though. She dialed my number but I wasn't there. She then dialed my cell phone and I answered.

"What are you doing this weekend?" Imani asked before I even said hello.

"I'm in Atlanta with Darrell. We are going to be here all weekend." I answered.

"Why didn't you tell me you were going to Atlanta? You had me calling your house looking for you." Imani shot back, sounding really frustrated.

"I'm sorry. It was a spur of the moment plan. What's wrong Imani?" I asked.

She answered "Do you think Jaloni ever loved me? Why hasn't he tried to get me back?"

I felt bad about not telling her about Jaloni's visit. I told her I am sure Jaloni loves her. "Loves? You said loves? Why? Do you know something?" Imani began screaming so I decided to tell her about Jaloni coming to see me. I also told Imani about the talk that Jaloni and I had.

"I can't believe you kept that from me. What the hell is wrong with you? What did you tell him?" Imani continued to scream.

I told her I couldn't talk to her right now and that set her off.

"You had plenty of time to talk to Jaloni. Why are you doing this to me? Did I do something to you? I would never talk to your man about you." Imani shouted.

"What are you talking about?" I asked Imani. "Why are you yelling at me? I found Jaloni banging on my door, screaming. You know I never get into anyone's business."

"Well you picked a fine time to start. Jaloni may never talk to me again." Imani screamed before she hung up the phone on me.

Imani was so mad. "To hell with all of them!" She thought

133

and then she yelled it out loud. Yeah, she is definitely going out this weekend and going to find her a new man. Maybe she would pick up a couple of friends while she is out.

Imani's mind began wandering now. She was wondered what Jaloni and I talked about. She also wondered why she couldn't trust anyone in her life. She assured herself that I was just jealous of Jaloni and her relationship and she didn't need jealous females in her life. She decided I am no longer her friend.

Darrell must have come in the room while Imani was yelling at me. I didn't hear him but when I turned around after hanging up the phone there he was. He asked me what is wrong and I told him nothing.

"Any nothing that makes your face look like is one I need to know about." Darrell said and stood waiting for an answer. "Is it something I have done?"

"No, of course not. This weekend is perfect. Imani and Jaloni are going through some things and I feel like they are putting me in the middle of it. That's all. Nothing to worry about or that will ruin our time here." I answered him, giving him a fake smile to indicate that everything is OK.

Darrell wasn't buying it at all. "You're not going to tell me what is going on? Come on, it will make you feel better." Darrell asked.

He sat down on the bed and offered me his lap as a seat.

I began telling Darrell about Jaloni and Imani's relationship. I explained to him how Imani always told everyone that she only fooled around on Jaloni because he did it to her. I told him I always thought it was true until Jaloni came to see me a couple of weeks ago and we talked. Jaloni swore on his father's grave that he has never cheated on Imani.

"Imani called me just then and asked me if I thought.

Jaloni ever loved her. I had kept my conversation with Jaloni a secret because I didn't want to get into it. Now Imani is mad at me, saying if Jaloni never speaks to her again it is my fault." I continued.

"Did you feel Imani should have known that you talked?" Darrell asked.

He looked very serious so I knew he was listening.

"I don't know. I just didn't want to get involved. I still don't want to get involved. I only told Imani because she asked me." I answered.

"Are keeping anything else from Imani?" Darrell asked.

"Don't make it seem like I was intentionally keeping information from her." I retorted and gave Darrell a stern look for his question.

"No, I'm not suggesting that at all. I'm asking you this because if you have told her everything, your hands are clean and they have to figure it out on their own." Darrell hesitated as he answered me and gave me a kiss on the forehead.

"Look at you; you were getting all mad at me. It is cute but I don't ever want you to be mad at me." He continued.

I just looked over at Darrell and smiled. This brought a smile to his face. He asked me if we were good and began trying to make a move on me.

"I don't know if we are that good. I said to Darrell as he began kissing my neck.

"Why? I've been good. I even listened to your problem. Don't I deserve something?" Darrell asked pouting like a child.

"So that is the only reason that you listened to me, to get brownie points and other perks?" I asked him.

I kept dodging his kisses.

Darrell answered, "No that is not the only reason. I listened to your problem because I care and I wanted to get that worried look off your face. Nookie is a mere after thought. You are sitting on my lap in a towel; it was bound to come up."

I laughed at Darrell. He is right and I felt it too. I gave in to him and he slipped me off of his lap and onto the bed. Before he started undressing me he gave me the "Are you sure look" and waited for my response. My response was pulling him closer, kissing, and undressing him.

CHAPTER 21

Imani is determined to go out. She went to the mall, bought a new outfit, one that would let the guys know what she had to offer. She spared no expense and the outfit left nothing to the imagination. She thought about calling Destiny to go out with her but quickly decided against it. The last thing she needed was to hear Jaloni's or my name. Imani decided to put all of us out of her mind and have a good time tonight.

She headed up to Saugus to one of her favorite spots. There are male exotic dancers performing and that always gets Imani in the mood for finding a fine black man. She arrived at the club and took a deep breath. She is not accustomed to going out alone.

Another thing she is not accustomed to is standing in line. It was cold out there and too many females looking at her whispering. She stood there because she knew she couldn't use the Jaloni Johnson's girl card anymore. Boston is so small. She knew the news of their breakup is bound to be common knowledge by now.

Imani had no idea what to do once she got in the club. She decided she couldn't go wrong with walking around. She got the majority of her attention by doing this in the past. Walking around she noticed there weren't many men in the place, certainly none that were of her caliber. Then she remembered the show. She proceeded to the area where the show was and found a seat. As soon as she did a group of females came up to her and told her she is in one of their seats.

Imani's first thought was to jump bad. That is always Imani's first thought. She didn't though because she remembered that she was there alone. She picked up her fur coat and walked off. As she walked by one of the girls attempted to trip her. Imani just smiled and kept walking. She continued to smile because she knew their actions were out of jealousy and that she still got it.

One of the dancers came out and saw Imani at the bar. He licked his lips and went directly to her. He slid up her, almost spilling her drink. She didn't care though. She liked the attention. She also liked the way he felt. It made her realize that it had been a while since she has been with anyone. The last time she had any male contact was a month before she left Jaloni.   She thought "I definitely need to get some tonight; I hope there are some fine men in here tonight. I'll let him drive the Beemer and then he can drive me." When she snapped back to reality, she realized the dancer is still there, grinding on her. She gave him an irritated look. He got up and left after realizing Imani's face showed she was no longer amused.

She sat at the bar for the majority of the night. Mainly because the girls who wanted the seat she was in were still giving her dirty looks. She thought about going to the VIP room and paying to get in. She went to the door and the bouncer recognized her. "Hey Imani." He said, pulling the rope to the VIP up for her to go in. She couldn't believe it. She thought she would have to pay to get in.

Actually she found out she would have to pay in another way. She was in there for about a half hour and the bouncer that let her in came over and began talking to her. "So how have you been?" He asked coyly. "I see you are still as fine as ever. Jaloni must be a fool" There is that name. She was hoping not to hear it tonight. He continued, "Well, he'll recognize it when he is in cold ass Utah and there are only them big boned Eskimos to keep him warm." Imani asked him what he is talking about. He told her Jaloni was traded to Utah today. Imani's heart dropped to her shoes. Now he is leaving town without saying goodbye. She ran out of the club but didn't know where she was going.

Imani drove around aimlessly before realizing she had nowhere to go. I wasn't in town and Jaloni was sure to be gone. She drove by his house just to make sure. His truck was nowhere in sight. There were lights on in the house but Imani remembered they came on automatically at 9 o'clock at night.

Imani thought about calling her parents but it was too late. Calling them would only make them worry. She thought about it, realizing she hadn't even told them she and Jaloni were no longer together.

Imani snapped out of her thoughts, realizing she is still parked in front of Jaloni's house. She spun off, hoping no one saw or recognized her or her car. She didn't understand why the news of Jaloni being traded affected the way that it did. She broke up with him and for the most part she is happy with her decision. They had no future. Imani knew it.

"Denise! Pick up! Pick up the damn phone!" Jaloni yelled into the answering machine. After a couple of seconds he said sorry. He was about to speak again when the answering machine cut him off. He thought of calling back, explaining what happened. Then he thought against it. It had been months since he last spoke to Imani. He sometimes believes he is happier without her but that thought only lasts about a second.

Jaloni did not want to be in Utah. He still couldn't believe he was traded. The team told him that they were going into a rebuilding phase and wanted younger players. The Celtics tried to sell Utah to him, telling him he has the chance to win a championship there. Utah's general manager was trying to relate the same bull to him earlier today.

"Why now?" Jaloni thought. He is just about to make his move to get Imani back. He figured whatever was bothering her is probably forgotten by now. Then he began thinking it is faith. That possibly Imani is not the one for him. Why else would all of these things happen? He thought that he would forget about her in time and he had to move on with his life. Utah, he thought again. He still didn't like the sound of it.

He sat down and looked out the window. He saw the snow on the ground and closed the blinds. He wondered what Imani was doing. He thought she was probably out parading around town. He wondered if she knew he was traded. She was never one for watching the news, especially not sports. Jaloni remembered having to almost force her to watch his games. She came around though he thought. She even came to a few. The thought brought a smile to his face.

Jaloni thought out his next move. Utah is definitely a drawback, he thought but he still believed that it is possible to get Imani back. He had to at least take a shot. He'd be better prepared to move on with his life if he knew whether or not they could be together.

Jaloni took out his Palm but had no idea of what was going on in that thing. It was a gift from his agent and his agent is the only one that uses it. He put all of Jaloni's important dates and set up meetings for Jaloni through it. It reminded Jaloni where to be and at what time but Jaloni could not use it to plan things himself.

Jaloni called his agent when he got so frustrated he almost threw it across the room. His agent asked if he knew how late it is. Jaloni did not. He let his agent know he had no idea what time it is in Utah or Boston then apologized for calling so late. His mind wasn't processing time or anything else but getting Imani back.

Jaloni asked his agent for the itinerary and could hear his agent sucking his teeth. His agent tiredly reached over and got his Palm and read the information off to Jaloni. Jaloni was happy when he heard he had two days before he could actually play a game for Utah. That would give him enough time to come up with some sort of plan.

Destiny still hadn't heard from Stephon. She called his house but got no answer. She was done trying. She figured it is really over. She picked up the phone to call one more time but for some reason she dialed Helena's number. Helena picked up the phone and Destiny lit into her.

"Well bitch, you got what you wanted." Destiny told Helena.

"Excuse me?" Helena questioned Destiny, "Who the hell do you think you are talking to like that?"

"You! Why couldn't you leave well enough alone? Stephon is gone now." Destiny answered.

"I would say I am sorry to hear that but I am not." Helena told Destiny.

Destiny couldn't believe what Helena said.
"What?" Destiny asked.

"You heard me. I can't say I am sorry." Helena answered. "I'm not going to apologize for doing what I could to keep you in my life. I will apologize for hitting you. I didn't mean to do that."

"Why are you making this difficult for me?" Destiny asked.

Helena's answer to Destiny's question was, "I'm not making anything difficult for you. You are making it difficult for yourself because you are denying yourself what you want."

"What am I denying myself? I want Stephon. I love him." Destiny exclaimed.

"You are denying me and your feelings for me. Come on Destiny I was there when we had sex, I know you have strong feelings for me." Helena told her.

"I love Stephon very much." Destiny responded.

"OK. Why are we having this discussion? Why call me at all? Go get him back." Helena suggested. "Or you can come see me and prove me wrong."

"Fine! I will." Destiny responded to Helena's suggestion.

"You will what?" Helena asked.

"Prove you wrong." Destiny answered. "I'll be there in twenty-five minutes."

Helena hung up the phone and didn't know what to expect. She certainly didn't expect Destiny to show up. About a half an hour past, Helena's doorbell rang. She thought to herself that it couldn't possibly be Destiny. She opened the door and there stood Destiny.

Helena opened the door wider to let Destiny in the house. Destiny stepped in the door and kissed Helena. Helena stood in shock until Destiny slapped her across her face.

"What the hell! Are you crazy?" Helena asked Destiny. "Why did you slap me?"

"Now we are even." Destiny told Helena.

Helena just looked at Destiny. She began to worry because she didn't know what Destiny would do next. Destiny grabbed Helena by her neck, pulling her right up to her face.

"What do you see?" Destiny asked Helena.

"I see you have lost your mind. Let me go." Helena told her.

"Why? Isn't this what you want?" Destiny asked before she kissed Helena again.

Destiny still had Helena by the neck and Helena kept attempting to break free.

"Stop it Destiny. You're hurting me." Helena said.

Destiny let her go with a shove. She looked at Helena, asked her what happened to her toughness. Destiny reminded her of how bold she was in the club. Helena told Destiny she is sorry for hitting her again and that she didn't mean to hurt her. She stepped closer to Destiny and reluctantly pulled her close. She wrapped her arms around Destiny and held her.

"I am sorry about your boyfriend." Helena told Destiny. "I didn't realize how much pain I caused you."

Helena kissed Destiny on the cheek. Destiny looked at her but didn't respond. Helena kissed Destiny again but on the lips.

"You don't understand how much you mean to me." Helena told her. "I got into a situation I can't control when I met you. I told you I love you."

Destiny still didn't answer Helena. Helena began playing in Destiny's hair. She took it out of the ponytail that Destiny had it in and just ran her fingers through it. Helena then pulled Destiny over to the couch and they sat down. Helena put Destiny's head on her chest and continued playing in her hair.

Destiny began to feel confused. She thought she has nothing else to lose. Stephon has already left her. She looked up at Helena and kissed her. Helena tried to stop Destiny. Destiny grabbed Helena by her hands. She pinned Helena's hands down and kissed her.

"You don't want this." Helena told Destiny.

Destiny shh'ed Helena, kissed her again.

"You love me right?" Destiny asked Helena.

Helena answered, "Yes. I love you very much."

"So make love to me." Destiny told Helena.

Helena stared at Destiny. She couldn't believe the 360 turn

143

she made since they talked on the phone. She really didn't want to go there with Destiny again but she wanted to be with Destiny. Destiny looked up at Helena again before undressing her.

Helena went along with it. They made love. Helena was so mad at herself. She didn't want to go through this cycle with Destiny. She looked at Destiny; she looked like she is in shock or something. Helena wanted to ask her what is wrong but she didn't want to hear the answer.

When Destiny snapped out of it she told Helena she had to go. She kissed Helena and began getting dressed. Helena didn't ask where she had to go or what is wrong. She just let her go. Helena knew that is all she could do is let Destiny go. Destiny told Helena she loves her before she ran out the door. Helena didn't respond because she knows it's not true.

CHAPTER 22

I'm home. Let the fun begin. I can feel trouble on the horizon like an arthritic person can feel the rain coming. The fact that I had so many messages on my phone and almost everyone knew I was going to Atlanta is also a strong indicator of the drama level. I thought positive thoughts, like thoughts of Atlanta. Atlanta was so much fun I didn't want to come back. Darrell didn't help matters by asking me to stay. I guess I could have stayed for a week but not forever like Darrell wanted. He did spoil me as promised.

I'm started smiling just thinking about the weekend I had. The smile was wiped away when the phone rang.

"Hello?" I answered the phone in a low suspicious tone.

"Damn girl! You don't sound like a person that just spent the weekend in Atlanta with a fine man. What, he didn't give you any?" Destiny asked trying to sound genuinely worried but her nosiness was evident.

"Very funny, Destiny. I thought you were Imani or worse Jaloni." I answered in an exhausted voice. "I don't know how I got in the middle of their nonsense. It seems like they are both blaming me for their shit."

"Don't worry about it and definitely don't talk to them. They'll figure it out on their own." Destiny said cheerfully. "Enough about them. So how was your trip?" Destiny is demanding all details.

I told her about the trip and how beautiful Atlanta is. I told her that Darrell's club is fantastic and was packed on Saturday night. I added that Darrell got jealous because some guy was trying to talk to me. She laughed, saying I am always starting trouble because I could have told the guy I was with someone.

"Atlanta is beautiful. There are black people everywhere. There were even black people in the spa. Not one or two of them, a lot of black people were in there. Darrell's house is beautiful. It is huge and so is his yard. He lives in a subdivision in a town outside of Atlanta called Alpharetta." I told her.

I continued by telling her that I was expecting to see a lot of white people where he lived because he lives so far from the city but there were black people everywhere in subdivision. There was even a brother out riding a lawnmower. Not something you would see in Boston. I could hear the excitement in my voice so I know Destiny could.

"Don't be trying to leave me. I'm watching you." Destiny said.

Yep. She heard the excitement in my voice.

She continued by saying that she'd get Darrell if he tried to take me away from her.

I continued by telling her he took me to one of the most beautiful malls, Phipps Plaza in Buckhead. He also took me to another mall, The Perimeter Mall, where I shopped like a crazy person and then we ate at Maggiano's.

"Destiny, I love that city and I love Darrell." I said and looked around like someone else could hear me. I haven't told Darrell yet.

"What? My girl is in love? For real? Did you tell Darrell? I know how you get." Destiny snickered like a kid with a secret.

"No I haven't told him. I just thought of it on the plane home. I was sad to leave and I was thinking about the whole trip." I told her.

I got sad just mentioning coming home.

"Girl you better tell him. But once again don't be trying to leave me." Destiny warned.

We talked a little while longer before I told her I had to get some rest. I felt jet-lagged and worried about Imani. I didn't know whether or not to call her so I decided I would sleep on it and try to call her tomorrow.

After getting off the phone with Destiny I checked my messages. There were three from Jaloni. I was thinking damn I don't want any part of their nonsense and Imani isn't even talking to me so what could he want. The third message explained it all. Jaloni was in Utah. Traded? Damn, I didn't know they could do that in the middle of the season.

I called Darrell on the phone and asked if someone can be traded in the middle of the season.

He said "Yeah. Why do you ask? Is Tyrone gone?"

"No it's not Tyrone. It's Jaloni. I guess that is why I had that discussion with Imani on Friday. I hate being in the middle of their nonsense but I am worried about Imani. She can't be taking this well." I answered. I realized that Darrell asked me if it was Tyrone and began laughing.

"What's so funny?" He asked.

"You! Are you still worried about Tyrone after the weekend we had? I apparently didn't do my job." I said in a seductive voice.

"No you did a very good job the whole time, you can come back any time you want to. I was just asking." Darrell said.

He began laughing also.

He continued, "I'm sure you have been nothing but a friend to Imani. I know you are worried but you see that helping them only gets you blamed for their lack of communication and problems."

I thanked him for listening and told him that I would say hello to Tyrone for him. He sucked his teeth and told me that isn't funny. He also said that we wouldn't be apart for long and that he loves me. I was quiet for a minute. I thought about it, told him that I love him too. He asked if I was for real and I told him always. He laughed at that. I told him I needed to get to sleep and I would call him tomorrow. We said good night and hung up.

I'm not panicking. I told Darrell I loved him and I didn't combust. I am not at all afraid. Damn this feels good. I went in the bathroom to take a shower but decided to take a bath. I ran the water and found some PJs to wear to bed. I smiled the whole time thinking about being in love with Darrell. I thought it would be a long time before I trusted anyone after Tyrone but I trust Darrell and I love him.

CHAPTER 23

Jaloni called his financial planner as soon as he arrived in Boston. He asked him to free up $100,000, telling him he needed it today. His advisor told him he wouldn't be able to do it. Jaloni yelled into the phone, "Do it or you are fired!" His advisor asked what time he needed it by. Jaloni said 3 o'clock.

His advisor shook his head because he knew the only way to do this was to take it from the firm's account which is held for client emergencies. He knew he would have to do it because the firm would not want to lose someone who makes as much as Jaloni does.

"Mr. Johnson, may I inquire what you need the money for? Maybe I can be of some assistance." He asked Jaloni. He was hoping it is for something that he could talk Jaloni out of like a car or some jewelry.

"The money is for someone special." Jaloni replied, telling him he would call back at three before hanging up the phone. He didn't give his advisor the opportunity to ask any more questions.

Jaloni found Janice's number. Janice is someone Jaloni dealt with in the past. She has helped him plan parties and events for his charity. He knew she could be trusted. He called her and asked her to meet him for lunch. She suggested a small Italian restaurant, citing she had a short lunch due to the amount of work she had to do. Jaloni agreed to meet her there.

Jaloni got dressed and headed to the mall. He had to find something very special and very expensive for what he had planned. He went to several stores, finally finding what he was looking for. He asked if the store could deliver it and the clerk responded yes. He paid down on it, telling the clerk he would return later with the rest of the cost and the address it should be delivered to. Jaloni made a couple more stops before he went to meet Janice.

Jaloni met Janice at noon at the restaurant she chose. At lunch, Jaloni noticed a man kept staring at him. After a while, he pulled out a pen and dangled it in the air to let the man know he would sign an autograph. The man didn't budge. Jaloni thought it was weird but didn't think anything of it. He just continued discussing his plans with Janice.

Jaloni told Janice, "Take the rest of the day off. Take the year off if you get hassled, I will pay your salary." She stared at Jaloni in amazement.

Janice told Jaloni. "There are no worries and I won't get hassled. I just hope your plan works. I'll do anything to help you." Janice said, still smiling at Jaloni.

He asked her, "Are you going to be able to get everything done by eight tonight?" She responded, "Yes as long as you can do the things you have to do. I'll go back to work now, fake being sick and get right on it."

She got up, hugged Jaloni, and told him how happy she is for him and how she hoped it worked out before she exited the restaurant.

Jaloni got so excited he almost left the restaurant without paying the bill. He had so much on his mind he just got up and headed for the door. The waiter who waited on his table came up to him and began talking. Jaloni assumed he wanted an autograph so he told him not now.

The waiter made Jaloni aware he didn't pay the bill. Jaloni

looked at the waiter for the longest time. What the waiter said still wasn't registering. The waiter pulled the bill out of his pocket, handing it to Jaloni. Jaloni laughed and said, "Oh why didn't you say so."

The waiter gave Jaloni a dumbfounded look and awaited Jaloni's payment. Jaloni took out a hundred dollars, telling him make sure he got the amount left over after the bill amount for his trouble. The waiter smiled at Jaloni, thanking him a few times after he looked at the bill and realized that it was only $17.

━━

Paul returned from lunch and went right to Imani's desk.

"I thought you told me that Jaloni got traded to Utah?"

Imani struck him a "not now" look but Paul continued,

"I just saw him in the restaurant with a woman. They seemed pretty close, hugging each other."

Paul did this partly to inform Imani and partly to push her closer to him. Imani just continued to stare at Paul.

She finally managed to say, "Jaloni is a single man. I can't control his actions anymore, nor do I desire to."

She sounded so sincere Paul walked off frustrated.

Imani just sat there, knowing she really wanted to cry. Imani wondered why he is here and why would he be with a woman?

About four o'clock Imani got a dozen red roses and a card. She looked around to see if Paul was watching her. It had been a while since he sent her flowers but he probably believed she needed them today. She opened the card and it wasn't signed.

It is more of an invitation than a card. The invitation

invited her to the party of the year. It stated that she is a special VIP guest and would be treated as such. The address on the invitation was Dynasty Ballroom's so she figured it is from one of the many promoters that she met over the years.

This excited Imani. It is just what she needed to get Jaloni and today's Jaloni update out of her head. Her thoughts then turned to what she would wear and what would she do with her hair. She knew she needed to go to the mall and salon so she went into her boss' office, told her that she isn't feeling well. Her boss said, "By all means go home and sleep it off then." Her boss just smiled because she got an invitation also.

Janice checked in with Jaloni at five o'clock. She informed him that Imani received her invitation to the party of the year and everyone else got an invitation also. She asked if he did his part and he answered cheerfully, "You know it. The ballroom is booked."

"I knew Imani couldn't resist a party and her boss said she left early, saying she didn't feel good. I bet if I called her salon she would be there." Janice told him and let him know that she had a couple more errands to run but they should meet at Dynasty at 7:30 p.m. to make sure everything is to his liking. He agreed and said, "Peace out."

I received my invitation around 4 o'clock. It insisted that I come early and have dinner with some of the other VIPs. I was wondering what this is and why I am VIP. Darrell called me to make sure I would come. He also told me to call Destiny and make sure she is coming.

I asked what is going on and he blew me a kiss through the phone before telling me he loved me but had to go. "See you tonight beautiful." I still get chills every time he calls me beautiful.

I feel so blessed and so happy to be with Darrell.

Destiny's phone rang forever. I wondered where she could be. She answered the phone out of breath and irritated.

"Were you busy?" I asked.

"Very funny. What do you want? Make it quick."

I asked her if she received an invitation to a party tonight. She said no but she would go check. She had been tied up all day.

"That is too much information!" I yelled and told her to go check. I heard her telling someone in the background that she would be right back. She came back to the phone and asked me what this is about. I told her I had no idea but Darrell called to make sure we were coming.

"Are you going Destiny?" I asked.

Destiny responded, "You know my nosy ass will be there."

She told me she had to go and we ended the conversation.

Jaloni was bouncing off the walls when Janice saw him at 7:30. "Calm down before you have a heart attack. You'll be no good to anyone if that happens." She was laughing so hard she spit her gum out. Jaloni didn't find it funny and a roll of his eyes alerted Janice to that fact.

He looked around at the ballroom and thought it is perfect. He asked Janice if she checked to see if everyone is coming. She told Jaloni she had Darrell check with Denise and Destiny because she didn't want them to get suspicious.

He said, "Right. Right."

He still looked like he wanted to vomit, bouncing from one foot to the other.

"What about Imani? Did you check with her to see if she is coming?" He asked in a more serious tone.

"I checked the salon and she is there. I told them to give her the works and I would send over a certified check to cover it. I told them if she asks any questions just tell her it is a special or something." Janice replied.

═══════════════════════════════════

      I decided to pick Destiny up. Just to make sure she made it. I got to Destiny's house and she and Stephon were still getting ready. I was surprised to see him there because the last time I spoke to Destiny she didn't know where they stood. I was also glad to see him there because I think he is good for Destiny.

      They are so cute I thought to myself and must have continued to smile because Destiny asked me why I am grinning like that. I told her I was just thinking about us, and all the things we have been through together. "That made you smile. You are a sick bird." Destiny said and returned my smile. Destiny walked over and gave me a hug.

"You know I love you right?" Destiny asked.

"Yeah." I answered.

      Then I told her to stop before she made me mess up my make up. Stephon also told Destiny to stop because she still isn't dressed. He told her to hurry up so we wouldn't be late. She rolled her eyes and then smiled at Stephon before she went to finish getting dressed.

═══════════════════════════════════

At the ballroom I noticed a few cars around but not enough for a party. Some of the cars looked familiar but I thought it is just a coincidence. Darrell's at the door, holding it down like the first night I met him. He looks just as good too. He had the black fur on, a blue pin striped suit under it. "What's a good-looking man like you doing standing out here all alone?" I asked and winked at Darrell. He played it off and looked around like he is looking for the person I am talking to.

Jaloni greeted us inside the ballroom. I looked at him and said, "Damn! What are you doing here? You look good Jaloni. How have you been?"

Jaloni had on a black Tux and is grinning from ear to ear.

He grinned and said, "I'm much better now. I'll explain everything during dinner. Your seats are marked. One thing I have to tell you. Tyrone is here with his wife."

I told him I am fine with that and he hugged me so tight he picked me up off the ground. I really am OK with Tyrone and his wife being here, although I still had no idea why I was here.

Destiny started, "What is Jaloni up to? I thought you told me he was traded or something like that."

Stephon confirmed that Jaloni was traded to Utah.

"Utah? What the hell is in Utah? They have a basketball team? So what is he doing here?" She looked around and didn't see Imani.

"I see he didn't invite Imani." She kept looking around and saw Imani's mother and said, "Damn, even her mother turned against her."

She continued to look around and saw Tyrone. "Isn't that the trifling Negro that Imani and Jaloni set you up with? Is that his wife? She is not pretty at all." I told Destiny to stop it but she couldn't. Destiny began laughing, getting loud. "Shouldn't you go over and say hi? Don't be so rude and don't forget to ask about mama."

She couldn't contain her laughter as she said that last part. She laughed so loud people began to look our way. Tyrone glanced over as well.

At dinner, Jaloni explained why we were there. He told us that he coordinated this surprise because he loves Imani and can't imagine living without her. He then asked Imani's father for Imani's hand in marriage. Imani's father gave Jaloni his blessing. Jaloni then got serious and began delegating roles.

Jaloni looked so content and comfortable. I wondered about Imani. I know she doesn't like surprises but I also know she wanted to marry Jaloni. The past few months have been hard for her but I know her feelings for Jaloni are still strong. I know this because of the way she blew up at me on the phone. I love her and wish them the best.

CHAPTER 24

Imani examined herself in the mirror. She definitely liked what she saw. She wondered who is throwing the party and if there is going to be a lot of fine men at the party. There must be for invitations that looked like that to be sent. She also wondered why her invitation came with roses.

The whole thing had her imagination peaked but she was ready for anything. She definitely needed the distraction. She checked her hair. Perfect! The black dress she wore was perfect. The dress was full coverage except for the fact that it was see through almost everywhere except where the velvet embroidery is intentionally placed.

On the drive to the ballroom, she let her mind wander. She thought of all the fine men that would be there tonight. She began thinking that there was probably going to be athletes in the place. She could definitely go for one of those. She thought to herself that she would just replace the old one with a new one. She laughed at the thought and laughed even louder when she imagined Jaloni seeing her out with one of the Patriots or one of his former teammates.

She pulled into the parking lot and saw that there weren't many cars. She thought that it is strange but figured there is a game on or something. Men tend to come later when there is a fight or game on TV. She had no idea who could be playing because she hadn't even watched sports since she broke up with Jaloni. From the emptiness of the parking lot, she believed it had to be the Patriots. She figured that it wouldn't be this deserted for a Celtics game. She continued through the parking lot to the ballroom.

Darrell was standing at the front door.

"I should card you but you look so good I'll let you slide." He told her. She told him to watch it because she still knows Denise's number. He told her point taken, have fun tonight and stay out of trouble. "I will not stay out of trouble," Imani said with a smirk as she walked down the hallway toward the VIP ballroom.

She walked in and thought she was in the wrong place. It looked more like a wedding reception than a party. There were cream-colored roses and carnations everywhere. In addition to the roses and carnations, there were an abundance of lilacs. She thought it is beautiful because of how much she loves Lilacs. She thought it is perfect and exactly how she would want the reception hall at her wedding when she got married.

She turned to leave because she knew she had to be in the wrong place. She thought she would at least ask Darrell where the party is or if she is too early. Then Imani heard someone call her name. She saw Jaloni and continued walking toward the door.

"Will you hold up Imani? I have something to tell you." Jaloni yelled behind her.

She looked at him, what he had on and asked if he was getting married.

He smiled and said, "I hope so. That is what I wanted to talk to you about."

"Congratulations Jaloni. That didn't take long."

Is all she could bring herself to say. He was thrown off guard by that and asked what she was talking about.

"Paul saw you in the restaurant with; I guess your fiancée today."

Jaloni began laughing and Imani began walking off.

He thought out loud, "That is the guy that kept mad dogging in the restaurant. Still looking out for the one he can't have. That's sweet."

Jaloni snapped back to reality in time to tell her Paul is wrong and ran to catch her.

When he caught up to her, he grabbed her by both of her hands and she tried to tug away.

"Jaloni let me go! I don't want to hear anything you have to say. This is sick." Imani demanded. She was still thinking Jaloni invited her to his wedding.

"Stop for one minute and I will explain." He asked.

Imani stopped, thinking maybe she should hear him out, it may be interesting. Jaloni got on one knee and Imani began fighting him again. "Will you marry me?" He asked, kissing her around her belly button. He let go to pull out the ring and she tried to run.

Jaloni reached out and grabbed Imani by the waist. He picked her up to guarantee that she didn't run again.

Imani looked at Jaloni in disgust and said, "We never talked about marriage Jaloni. You told me no one would marry someone like me."

She was still trying to get away.

He apologized for all of that, telling her she frustrated him at times but he could live with it. He also told her he couldn't live without her and he loved her from first sight and will always love her.

"Will you marry me?" He asked again.

She wanted to say no so bad but thought of how long she has waited to hear Jaloni say those words.

She formed her mouth to say no but she said, "Yes. Yes Jaloni I will marry you."

He said, "Will you marry me right now?"

She looked at him like he is crazy.

"Oh my God! You sent me an invitation to my own wedding? What if I would have said no?" She asked cheerfully. "I have on black. What am I going to wear?" She was still smiling so Jaloni didn't think there is a problem. He smiled back at Imani, shrugged, pulled out his cell phone. Janice came out of the ballroom with a beautiful wedding gown. "Will that do?" He asked still smiling.

"This is all happening too fast." Imani began.

The smile left Jaloni's face because Imani stopped smiling.

"We aren't even together. You live in Utah now. I don't know if I can be with someone that is away that much. You were away enough when you played for the Celtics." Imani continued.

Jaloni just looked at Imani. He could feel his heart breaking in a million pieces as she spoke. He always said he didn't know what he would do without her. He started thinking he is going to have to find out. He looked around, not knowing what to say to Imani. Some time while she was talking, Janice had managed to leave with the dress. Jaloni would have to thank Janice for that later. He guessed Janice figured the dress would put too much pressure on Imani.

Jaloni pulled out the ring, showing it to Imani, mostly because he knew that Imani couldn't resist jewelry. He took her hand, slid it on her finger and held her finger in his hand. Jaloni didn't want to let it or her go. He really didn't know what to say to her. He just stood there, praying that she would come around.

"Take this." Jaloni told her. "At least let this be an engagement party. All your family and friends are here. We can talk about all of the details later. I will not accept no for an answer. You already said yes."

She looked up at him, for the first time she saw pain in his eyes. She thought to herself if she causes all of that pain? She always thought about her pain but didn't think about Jaloni's. She didn't even know that he was carrying all that pain around until I told her what he said when he visited me. Imani really didn't want to hurt Jaloni anymore so she slid the ring off her finger and dropped it on the floor before running out of the place.

CHAPTER 25

Jaloni came back in the ballroom and announced that there wouldn't be a wedding. He told everyone to enjoy the food and champagne and thanked them for coming. He looked like a dying man. His parents approached him first. His mom looked like she wanted to say something negative about Imani but withheld when his stepfather shot her a look. His stepfather just hugged him. Jaloni looked up and backed away from his stepfather.

He looked toward the DJ and asked why there isn't any music. The DJ changed the song he had cued because it is the song Jaloni picked for the first dance. He then found something he believed would be more appropriate and began to play music.

Jaloni came and sat at our table. We all surrounded him. His face had "Why" written all over it but he didn't say anything. I asked where she went and he said, "She left the building, she is probably long gone." I got up and went to the door to see. Her car is still in the parking lot.

I took Darrell's coat off the hanger near the door and went to get her. She saw me coming and started the car. I didn't think she would drive with me walking directly in front of the car but the closer I got, I realized I was wrong. She hit me. That's all I remember.

Darrell ran over to see if I was OK. He watched as Imani sped away. He called an ambulance and waited out there with me until the ambulance came. The EMS' asked what happened. Darrell told them that a car hit me. As people from inside heard the sirens they came out to see what happened. I could hear people whispering but I couldn't move. I found out later that I couldn't move because I was strapped in the gurney.

Once I regained consciousness, I begged Darrell not to tell anyone that Imani hit me. Everyone began asking questions. The whispers got louder. Darrell had to tell everyone to move back because everyone had surrounded me. Jaloni stared at me like he knew exactly what happened and looked apologetic. Jaloni began pushing the EMT, telling them he wanted to come in the ambulance with me.

I was so scared in the ambulance. They wouldn't let Jaloni, Darrell, or Destiny ride with me because they are not family members. They gave them the information about where they were taking me before they pulled off. They took me to BWH in Boston or at least that is where I was when I woke up. I found out I had a concussion and a fractured fibula but nothing was broken. I woke to a lot of pain.

"They said to push the button for the pain medicine and that one for the nurse when you wake up." Darrell said.

I looked groggily over at him and said, "Hi."

"Why won't you let me tell the police Imani hit you?" He asked.

I gave him a look that said, "not now." I think. It might have just been so pathetic he decided to leave me alone.

"Where's Jaloni?" I managed to ask.

Darrell told me that Jaloni had to leave. He plays his first game tonight and has to report before noon to be eligible to play. I shook my head up and down to let him know I understood. Shaking my head hurt me almost as much as anything I had ever experienced. What hurt the most is realizing someone I believe is my friend could do this to me. She didn't even stop. Maybe Darrell is right. Maybe I should turn her in.

The phone rang and Darrell picked it up. There was silence on the other end. After asking 3 times who it is he turned to me and stated, "You know it's her right." I thought was at least she isn't so far gone that she didn't check on me. "Imani!" Darrell yelled before the person hung up. He ranted for a long time about her being wrong.

I couldn't say anything to defend her because I didn't understand why she hit me either. I asked Darrell to leave so I could get some sleep. "Absolutely not so that psycho chick can come and finish you off. I'm staying right here until visiting hours are over. I am not losing you." If he said any more than that I don't know because I drifted back to sleep.

I woke up to the same pain I had earlier. I started going crazy until I remembered I am supposed to push a button to get pain medicine. I looked up and Darrell was gone. "They must have thrown him out." I thought and turned back around.

I thought I heard a noise so I turned again and saw Imani coming at me. I was ready to press the nurse's button when she reached out. Darrell had me shook with that she wants to finish me off theory.

"I'm so sorry." She said while trying to hug me. I waved her off and she began to cry.

"Stop crying Imani. It doesn't become you." I stated and then tore in with, "Why the hell did you hit me?" She told me she didn't mean to hit me and she believed she had enough room to make it out of the parking space.

She apologized again saying she knows she shouldn't have left me there but she wasn't thinking clearly and didn't want to answer any questions. She went on to say she would never do anything purposely to hurt me.

"I just couldn't stop. When do you get sprung from here? I am going to take such good care of you." She said brightening up a little.

I just stared at her. She hits me then wants to take care of me. I really couldn't say anything to that.

"Jaloni?" I said, snapping her out of her fantasy world. "You hurt him really bad."

She looked at me like she had no idea what I was talking about.

Finally she said, "He is better off without me. He'll see. I hurt him too much."

She was actually smiling when she said it.

"How?" I asked drifting back to sleep but fighting to stay awake to hear her answer.

I must have lost that battle because that is the last thing I remember from that conversation. Imani was probably relieved that she didn't have to answer my question. She left a note on the nightstand saying she would be back in the morning with reinforcements and she loved me.

I came home three days later; Imani was at my front door, as promised, ready to take care of me. I had to keep reminding Darrell to drop it. "You're not needed here. Don't you have some other friends to run over with your car?" Darrell asked. I thought to myself that lasted all of twenty seconds.

I got in the house and there were 21 messages on my phone, five were from Jaloni. Imani looked sad when she heard his voice. By the third message she screamed, "OK enough, what does he want."

This set Darrell off again. He told her, "It's not his fault he has feelings and concern for a person that was left to die by a so-called friend."

"It's Jaloni's fault." Imani screamed. "What was he trying to prove with his shotgun wedding?"

Darrell said, "Yeah he is going to be much better off without you."

I looked at Imani who had to realize that I told Darrell she said that.

"Do you feel the same way Denise?" She hollered. "I never wanted to hurt Jaloni or you. He hurt me too. Did anyone stop to think about that? What about my baby?"

Darrell looked at her like she was crazy. That was something I didn't tell him.

"Baby, what baby? Are you...?" He asked in total confusion.

I interrupted him by moaning like I am in pain. He looked at me and when he was sure I wasn't in any immediate pain he turned back to Imani who was a pile on the floor.

While Imani was out, I explained everything to Darrell. She asked what happened when she came to. I told her that she fainted.

"I have to get out of here. I'll be back; do you need anything from the store?" Imani asked on her way out the door.

She was gone so fast. She was practically out the door before we could respond to her question.

Darrell told her to drive carefully. Both Imani and I shot him a look that could have cut glass. He changed it up and said. "Imani. Take care of yourself."

She looked at him and smiled, not knowing whether to be pleased or skeptical.

Imani arrived in Utah at 7:30 p.m. What made her come out to this cold place in the winter she thought? She knew exactly why she is here and isn't planning on leaving until she spoke to Jaloni. She went to the arena where Utah played their games but there were no players there. Imani began to question some of the employees but nobody would answer any questions for her. She argued that she is his fiancée but they wouldn't budge. She went back to the hotel and tried to figure out her next step.

Imani called me. I answered the phone and I believe that Imani was already talking.

"Remember how Jaloni called you all those times?" she asked, even before she said hello. "Do you have the number he called from?"

Imani still didn't say hello.

"Who am I speaking with?" I thought I would mess with her first. I actually have all of Jaloni's information. He left it on my voice mail the first time he left. She sucked her teeth but still didn't say who she was.

"How are you feeling?" she asked. I answered good and asked her why she wanted Jaloni's information. She told me she is ready to talk to him and clear everything up.

I gave her the information and she blew me a kiss through the phone. I tried to ask her what she is going to do and she just laughed and told me everything will be OK. She told me she loves me and hung up the phone.

Why did Imani need Jaloni's address, I thought. I didn't think to ask her that while she was on the phone. I also wondered would everything be OK and what she is going to say to him. I prayed for both of them before I went to sleep.

Jaloni sounded so depressed when he answered the phone. He sounded so bad Imani's heart dropped.

"Hello Jaloni."

When he heard Imani's voice he perked up.

"Hey, how are you? Have you seen Denise? How is she doing? Is she mad at you? I'm sorry." Jaloni asked Imani.

"Why are you sorry Jaloni?" confused by his apology. "We need to talk about what happened and why it happened."

He had mixed emotions about seeing her. He knew they needed to talk so decided he would. He agreed and told her he had so many questions he wanted to ask her. She told him where she was and Jaloni began to laugh. He asked where she wanted to meet and told her that he is in the same hotel. She laughed. "I've been searching for you for hours and you are in this hotel. I never thought to check here."

Imani and Jaloni talked for hours. They talked about everything. He told her about knowing about her cheating on him. She told him about the baby. The sun was coming up before they looked up. They smiled at each other and Jaloni told her that he had to go. "Will you be here when I get back?" he inquired. She shook her head no but promised they would talk again. His grin got wide as he walked off.

Jaloni left kind of relieved. His talk with Imani answered a lot of questions. He was especially interested about her stay in the hospital. He told her that he was saddened by the thought that someone would believe that he would put his hand on her. Jaloni was extremely saddened when she told him about the miscarriage.

He realized from their talk he pushed Imani away as much as she pushed him away. He didn't even remember saying most of those things to Imani. Jaloni apologized and told Imani that he would never talk to her like that again if she gave them another chance. She said she would think about it. Jaloni thought this is a start, a very positive start.

Imani headed back home to be with her family during Christmas. She realized that she didn't visit her family enough. Her visit would definitely be a surprise. The surprise was all hers, no one was home. She went over and asked a neighbor where they went. The neighbor told Imani they were on a vacation. Imani thought about calling Destiny or me to ask us what we were doing but decided she would spend Christmas alone. She needed the time to think anyway.

As soon as she walked in the door the phone rang. She heard Jaloni's voice on the other end and smiled. She was at peace with the progress they made during their talk. He was happy she answered because he wasn't able to be near his family for Christmas either. They talked for most of the day.

Jaloni looked at the clock, thought about how much he enjoyed talking to Imani and how much it was like when they first met. He got sad because he knew he had to go to practice and didn't want to hang up. He was already late and knew it would take him more than the 15 minutes he had left to get to practice. With him being new to the area they would just think he got lost or something. He told Imani he loved her and would see her soon and she reciprocated but didn't tell Jaloni she loved him.

Jaloni was all smiles and could care less about being late for practice. He felt all is right in his world at this moment. He thought to himself that all he had to do is keep his cool and he would get Imani back before he knew it. They have really gone through a lot and he felt they could make it through anything after this year

CHAPTER 26

It's New Year's Eve and I am so happy. This year cannot end quickly enough for me. I am not dressed yet, as usual I am running late. My leg still hurts at times but it is better. This year there will be no wild party, just us girls and Darrell and Stephon, getting together for a special event.

Imani and Destiny are going to kill me if I am late. I put on a blue dress and did my hair while Darrell patiently waited downstairs for me. I can imagine him nervously pacing back and forth. I began to laugh because he is always like that when we go out. He heard me laughing and asked what I am laughing at. I told him nothing and he sucked his teeth.

The limo was out front by the time I made it downstairs. I kissed Darrell on the cheek and asked if I am worth the wait. He looked me up and down and responded, "Let's hurry up and get out of this house before we don't make it at all. So was I right last year?"

"You were right about what?" I responded.

"I told you if you rang in the New Year with me you would end up with me," he answered while he nodding his head up and down.

I responded. "Is that what you are sticking around for? You can go now."

I laughed. He told me he wasn't going anywhere "ever."

The chapel was small; intimate just the way they wanted it. Only fifty people were invited to the wedding. Destiny, Imani, and I were in the back making sure everything is perfect. This time there is no cat walking. We just stared at each other.

"Well." I started. "Last year we toasted to trouble and we definitely got it. This year let's toast to something different. First. To the bride and groom."

"To the bride and groom." They repeated in unison.

"Secondly, to all the happiness we can stand." I said as we clanked glasses.

Imani and I left Destiny to make her final preparations. As we were going out the door, Helena was standing there. Imani went right for her. I stopped her and thought to myself we should have toasted to no more drama.

Imani made Helena promise not to start anything, telling her she would take her heels and earrings off if she had to. Helena looked frightened, shook her head up and down, acknowledging what Imani said. We walked off but kept looking back, listening every few seconds to see if we were needed.

Helena stepped in the dressing room and she couldn't contain herself. She just wanted to touch Destiny once. She saw a strand of hair hanging out of place and took her opportunity. Destiny jumped back and asked Helena what she was doing there.

"Goodbye. I just wanted to say goodbye." Helena exclaimed while she continued to stare at Destiny. Destiny didn't answer her. She didn't even look at her.

Helena took steps near the door and turned around to tell Destiny how beautiful she looked before leaving. Destiny thought everything she and Helena had to say to each other was said when she called and told Helena she was getting married.

Apparently Helena didn't think so. She only called Helena

as a courtesy and because she didn't want any drama if Helena heard it from someone else or saw the announcement in the newspaper. Destiny realized Helena must have seen the announcement, anyway because she didn't tell her where the wedding was going to be.

Destiny and Stephon's wedding was a short but elegant one. There were white lilies, roses, and carnations everywhere. It was the same thing at the reception hall. It was all planned out by Destiny; we didn't even know until we received our invitations by express mail.

Darrell and I called Destiny and got the low down as soon as the invitation came. Destiny told us Stephon proposed on Christmas day in front of her whole family. She had no idea he was going to propose but she was worried Stephon and her father were spending so much time together. She told us Stephon said her father took a while to give his blessing. Stephon was as surprised as the rest of them when her father announced Stephon had something to ask the family during dinner.

There was enough food to feed an army at the reception. Destiny spent more time with us than she did with Stephon until Imani brought it up. She told us it is because she hadn't seen us in weeks and didn't know when she would see us again. Imani answered "Like you could get rid of us. Tell Stephon we'll be over for dinner next week." She laughed and then told us about him getting a teaching position at the University of St. Louis. She said that is also the reason for the small, quick wedding.

We toasted to, "No more drama and her having lots of babies." She wasn't amused by the second part of the toast at all. We couldn't help but to laugh when her father toasted to the same thing. He wanted lots of grand babies, no matter how far away they were.

Imani got up to give a toast and I think everyone in the place that knew her held his or her breath. Some people covered their ears, I think. She toasted to longevity and success, saying that it needed to be worked at. She then told the bride and groom to never give up on each other. Everyone was shocked but began applauding Imani's toast.

The clock was about to strike midnight and I couldn't help but realize we were about to ring in the New Year together. "A wise and very fine man once told me if you ring in the New Year with someone, you'll spend the year with them. Here is to spending the next year and the rest of our lives together." That was the final toast of the year. We all laughed as we counted down the last ten seconds, thinking that the next year couldn't come fast enough.

Destiny made all of us dance with her and Stephon. It was the last dance of their reception but the first dance of the New Year. Imani and I danced together while Darrell took pictures, claiming he was going to blackmail us with them later. If he only knew the half of what happened this year he wouldn't even joke like that. But it is OK; we were all laughing about it.

Destiny got teary eyed and we told her to stop. Imani threatened to kill her if she messed up the makeup it took her almost an hour to do. Destiny didn't care and didn't stop crying. She knew in the matter of weeks she would be in St. Louis and we wouldn't be there with her.

"We spent a lot of time fighting and arguing and now we are going to be apart. I'm sorry for everything. I love you two. You are my sisters." Destiny said. Destiny's real sister poked her in the side when she said that. Destiny smothered her in return.

Destiny continued, still holding her sister tight. "OK. Y'all are my other sisters. I love you and thank you for the love and patience that you have showed me this year. Imani, I wish you all the luck, love, and joy that you can stand. I know it's not much but

I wish it upon you anyway." She began laughing. Imani looked at her like she didn't understand. "Don't look at me like you don't think love is smothering." Destiny continued. Imani got what Destiny was saying and started laughing with the rest of us.

"Denise, I wish you the same." She said and looked over at Darrell, told him not to make her come back here. "You have my oldest and closest friend's heart, take care of it. Destiny continued. Everyone was crying and laughing at the same time. Darrell rose his glass to Destiny, trying to play it cool. He looked one word away from crying himself.

Destiny was about to begin again when Stephon came and got her. He told her it is time to go greet the other guests as they exited. He kissed her; we all awed and oohed at them. Stephon said, "What? I married her first." We all laughed at that and waved bye to Destiny as she went to take her place at the door of the reception hall.

We reenacted the whole dramatic scene again when we got to the door and had to say goodbye to Destiny. Stephon and Darrell looked at each other and shrugged. Darrell looked at Stephon and told him,

"I blame you. You are the one taking the third musketeer away."

Stephon's answer was, "I have to man. I love her. I have a feeling she will be back more than you think or on the phone. So get your personal time in now before she gets homesick or you may never get it."

We all waved and cried as they rode off in his SUV. They were going to spend the night at the airport hotel before they went off to their honeymoon. Destiny's family chipped in and got them a cruise Caribbean cruise. The cruise was going to last for twelve days and then they are coming back to Boston. We were so busy waving; telling Destiny to call us we forgot to throw our rice and Destiny momentarily forgot to throw her bouquet. They were all the way down the street when all of a sudden we saw the SUV backing up.

Everyone began to look worried when they first pulled up. Destiny stuck her head out of the window and said, "I guess I was supposed to do this inside. Stephon looked and saw I still had the bouquet in my hand and began backing up like a madman. He said it is bad luck for me not to throw it, so ladies line up."

Imani and I looked at each other, attempted to run the other way. Destiny alerted us to the fact that she saw us running and made us get in front. Imani and I must have had the same idea because we separated. Imani went one way and I went the other so she couldn't aim it at us. Imani ended up catching it anyway. She looked like she wanted to cry. Destiny just laughed and got back in the car. She blew kisses at everyone again and thanked them for coming as they drove off.

CHAPTER 27

When I woke up on New Year's Day Darrell was nudging me in my side. I rolled over to see what he wanted. I hoped he wants a repeat of last night's performance.

"What Darrell? Why are you nudging me like that?" I asked in a groggy annoyed voice.

"You don't know?" He asked me.

His annoyed tone matched mine. I was beginning to worry.

"No I don't know." I thought for a minute and then said, "Happy New Year baby."

I kissed him on his lips.

He laughed and then he said, "Your phone has been ringing all morning. How can you sleep through that?"

"Why didn't you answer it?" I asked him.

I was still groggy and I think he knew that.

He asked me, "Oh I got it like that? I can just answer your phone?"

"You, sexy, got it anyway you want it, anytime you want it." I answered.

Darrell stared at me for a moment and took my comment as exactly what it was; an attempt to throw him off track. He kissed me on the lips, then on my neck. He started to venture lower when the phone rang. He looked over at me but I didn't move so he picked it up.

Darrell answered the phone, "Hello. Denise's house."

I began cracking up in the background.

"Eww! What are y'all doing?" Imani asked Darrell. "Why did you answer the phone?"

Darrell looked confused for a moment and then he gave me the phone. He didn't tell me who it was or say anything. He just handed the phone to me.

"Hello?" I asked I was still laughing.

"Y'all so nasty. Why did you answer the phone while you are getting it on?" Imani asked.

I could only imagine what she said to Darrell.

"Ain't anybody getting it on, crazy? What did you say to Darrell?" I asked.

Imani told me she asked him the same thing. I couldn't help laughing. I told Imani to hold on and turned over to kiss Darrell.

After I kissed him Darrell asked me, "What was that for?"

"Like I need a reason?" I answered as I picked the phone back up.

Darrell just looked at me like I was keeping a secret from him. Then he got up and left the bedroom.

"Hello!" Imani started screaming through the phone.

"What Imani?" I asked.

"You don't just leave people on the phone while you do your boyfriend. That's rude. Especially a friend that's not getting any." Imani retorted.

"We weren't doing anything. How many times am I going to have to tell you that?" I asked Imani.

She shot back, "Until I believe you heifer or never, whichever comes first." Imani burst out laughing before she continued. "OK! I believe you. You could have let a sista embellish or at least think one of us is getting some."

Imani got quiet on the phone for a minute. When she spoke again she said, "You know it doesn't count."

"What doesn't count Imani?" I asked her.

I really had no idea what she is talking about.

"That I caught the bouquet. It doesn't count because she threw it at me." Imani sounded really serious now.

I couldn't help myself. I had to mess with her.

"She did not throw it at you." I said. I was lying. I thought that Destiny threw the bouquet at her too.

"Why are you freaking out?" I asked Imani after I regained my composure.

"I'm not. I'm just saying it doesn't count." Imani answered quickly. "Can you believe Destiny got married? And she would get married first? I thought for sure one of us would get married before Destiny." Imani still sounded serious.

"Which one of us?" I asked. "Me with my bad taste in men or you the runaway bride?"

We both laughed. I was actually surprised Imani laughed. She never wants to talk about that night. She rarely wants to talk about Jaloni, even though they are friends now. Almost like she was reading my mind Imani started,

"Jaloni is doing well. He told me to tell all of you and the rest of Boston Happy New Year."

"If you talk to him again, tell him I wish him the same." I answered hesitantly. I was still thinking it is spooky she knew I am thinking about Jaloni.

"He'll be here next month. Tell him yourself." Imani said snapping me out of my thought. "Naw. I'm just kidding. He will be here next month though. They play the Celtics on the February 12th. He also wants us all to go to dinner or something while he is here." Imani said.

Imani sounded almost sad when she said that. I left it alone though.

I looked up because I heard a noise. I forgot Darrell was here so I was even more shocked to see him standing there buck naked, with a tray of fruit and some other things I couldn't see. I told Imani I had to go and I would call her back. She called me nasty before she hung up the phone.

At least I think Imani hung up the phone. I didn't hang it up on my end and I began to hear that buzzing tone. I picked the receiver up and hung it up, staring at Darrell the whole time.

"What is this?" I asked.

"If you don't know what it is, I am definitely not doing my job." He answered grinning.

"I meant the tray." I answered.

I was still staring at him. It was the first time I have seen him completely naked, in full view. It was an amazing view. Usually we are already engaged in something by the time he gets to naked. He is beautiful. The more I stared at him, the more aroused he got.

He put the tray down, stood back up and continued to stand there. I got off the bed and went to him, staring at him the whole time. He was so aroused he moaned when I touched him. That was his only response. I got on my tiptoes, kissed him on the mouth. I was still touching his body, running my fingers all over, exploring him.

Darrell couldn't take much more and I knew it because he started trembling. I began to play with the creases between his muscles with my tongue. I got to his stomach and he came. Darrell looked down at me and then looked down at it.

He looked at it like it betrayed him or something. He was definitely shocked. I was too because I hadn't even touched it. I got up and kissed him. First, on his mouth, then on his shoulder. Then I led him over to the bed and the tray he prepared for me.

We got back into bed and I began picking at the fruit. I noticed there was some honey and whip cream on the tray with the fruit. I looked over at him and he was in full zombie mode. I took the whip cream and sprayed it on a strawberry and fed it to him. He just opened his mouth like an uncontrolled movement, taking the strawberry.

I know what is wrong with him but I didn't want to go there. I tried to feed him more fruit but he was unresponsive in every way.

"I'm sorry." Darrell spoke in the same zombie mode he is moving in.

"Sorry for what?" I asked.
I was serious.

"Sorry for reacting like a schoolboy getting his first piece. For disappointing you." He answered.

"You have nothing to be sorry about. You just owe me one." I said.

I laughed, he didn't. I thought to myself, I knew it wasn't the right thing to say but it came out anyway.

"Are you OK?" He asked.

"Yes I am fine. Why wouldn't I be?" I answered. "You're fine too. We're good."

He began to smile but he was still hesitant. I kissed him again on the lips, put my head on his shoulder and held him.

"You know there is nothing wrong with that or you. You think I didn't get anything out of it, you're wrong. I probably would have done the same thing if you touched me." I told him, hoping he would get over it.

"Yeah but you would have recovered a lot quicker." He answered.

That response let me know that Darrell is not going to get over it for a long time. It also let me know I am not going to get any. I picked at a couple more pieces of fruit and then got up and went in the bathroom. I decided to take a shower so I stuck my head out of the bathroom door to let Darrell know. He was gone. I yelled his name a couple of times but he didn't answer.

After I got out of the shower, I called his house. He didn't answer. I called the club, only to get the voicemail. I shook my head in disbelief. I couldn't believe this is affecting him like that. I wanted to talk to someone about it but the only person around is Imani and I would never do that to him. She would bring it up in front of him or make jokes to let him know she knew.

I couldn't talk to my mother about it. Damn my mother. I remembered I am supposed to go to her house for dinner and bring Darrell. What is she going to think if I show up without Darrell? I began thinking of excuses for why he couldn't make it when he walked back into the room.

"Hey." He said.

"Why didn't you tell me you were going out? Is everything OK?" I asked.

I hope the tone didn't sound standoffish.

"Yeah, I'm better now. I just had to clear my head. That has never happened to me before." He answered.

I couldn't help myself. I started laughing because that is always the line that guys use. Even, if it has happened to them before.

"What's so funny?" Darrell asked.

He looked like he wanted to bolt through the door again.

"Nothing I am sorry." I answered, went over, and grabbed him by his waist.

If he was going to run he was taking me with him. I thought about it for a minute, remembering he was a running back and probably could run with me attached to him easily. I looked up at him to make sure he was alright and not about to take off.

"Are you alright for real?" I asked to be sure.

He nodded his head, looking at me suspiciously.

"Do you still feel like going to my mother's house with me?" I asked.

He nodded again.

"What is that I feel?" I asked.

I really thought and was hoping it was what I thought it was.

"Oh, this. I got this for you. Happy New Year." He said as he shoved the box into my hands.

I opened the box and saw the charm. It is gold and appeared to be a baby. I looked at him, totally confused.

"It's the New Year's baby. At least that is what the guy who sold it to me told me." Darrell said laughing at my confusion and the fact he was probably ripped off.

"Oh. OK." I was still confused.

Darrell pulled another box out of his back pocket.

"What's this?" I asked.

"Open it." He answered.

It was a charm bracelet. He told me we are going to use it to commemorate every milestone in our relationship. He told me he loves me and thanked me for being so understanding about what happened. I was happy to get the gifts but now I was wondering if he got them out of guilt. I felt so bad for him because he is letting it eat away at him. I wanted so bad to help but I had no idea how.

I think my mom loves Darrell as much as I do. She told me he is fine, I almost lost it. Eww! I thought. My mother is checking out my boyfriend.

"See now you know I can't leave you alone with him. I'm not going to end up on Jerry Springer, trying to beat you down for sleeping with him." I said.

"Now you know better than that. He is way too young for me." She answered. "Furthermore he might kill me. Your mother's getting old."

I just laughed. Mainly because I thought she would slap me across the room for the Jerry Springer comment. I think she is just so happy that I found someone and Destiny getting married probably has her thinking I'm next. I hesitantly asked her about what happened earlier between Darrell and me.

"Oh child, that's just his pride. Give him some time and he'll get over it." She continued. "I hope. It would be a shame for all that to go to waste.

She is laughing at me. I am shocked and appalled.

"See if I ever come to you with a problem again. I am serious. He went out, bought me jewelry and everything. He is feeling very bad about it." I answered.

Ahh! The power of guilt I thought.

"I'm sorry baby. I didn't know." She answered. "He'll be OK, just stick with him and let him know that it is nothing to feel guilty about. Jewelry? Huh? Where is it?"

"It's a gold charm bracelet. I would never wear that. I don't think he expects me to either. It is to mark our milestones." I told her.

She just looked at me, smiling. She was so happy I am in love. She couldn't even hide it.

"Well we better go out there and get him before Jr. and the kids run him out of here.

        We went out in the living room and Darrell had both kids on his back as he crawled across the floor. Then he stopped and said, "They almost dropped me for a lost."

I had no idea what that meant but I laughed anyway. I looked at Jr. and he called the kids off. They got up and Darrell got up holding his back. I rushed to his side and he laughed.

"I'm fine. Dang, do you think I'm that old?" He asked laughing.

I didn't know what to say so I just laughed with him.

        At dinner, Darrell and Jr. talked about sports until my mother asked Darrell about our relationship.

"Do you plan on marrying my daughter?" She asked.

"Stop it." I said.

I almost spit out my food.

"Yes." Darrell answered. "I told your daughter I knew she was my wife from the moment I laid eyes on her."

"You stop it too." I told him.

I was totally embarrassed but they continued talking about it. I became even more embarrassed when Darrell told them how I fell for him literally. Even the kids were laughing at me. I decided I would go get the dessert so they could continue to talk about me.

Jr. followed me into the kitchen.

"Why didn't you want him to answer momma? Don't you feel the same about him?" He asked.

"I do. I just thought it was a line when he said it to me. I was shocked to hear him say it again." I answered. "Momma had no business asking him that anyway. I don't want to rush things."

"Oh I get it. You think it's going to be like the rest of your relationships? Let those go, deal with the present. He seems like a good man." Jr. told me before he snatched a piece of pie and ran back into the dining room.

Momma and Darrell were looking at me like I had eight heads and smiling when I got back in the dining room. I started thinking they have probably already planned the wedding. I found out Jr. told them they are making me nervous and to change the subject.

Jr. asked Darrell about all the women he met on the road. "Way to change the subject bro." Darrell looked at Jr. like he was crazy for asking that question.

He said, "I'm not answering that. Do I look stupid? Anyway that is far in my past and I only have eyes for one woman from now on."

He smiled at me and blew a kiss across the table.

"Game I tell you. All game." I answered his declaration. "But don't stop. I love it."

Everyone laughed but Darrell.

"I'm just kidding, baby. I'm sorry." I said.

He burst out laughing and said, "Gotcha!!"

I told momma we have to go because Darrell has some things to do at the club. He told Jr. to come by one night when he isn't locked down. Jr. laughed; said he won't be there anytime soon. My momma hugged Darrell as we went out the door.

"Jerry, Jerry!" I said and we both laughed.

Darrell looked confused but left it alone. She gave me a hug, told me to take care of myself and take care of Darrell.

She stood in the doorway, grinning as we drove off.

CHAPTER 28

"Did you miss me?" Destiny asked as soon as I picked up the phone.

"You know I did. Damn two whole weeks. What am I going to do when you are gone?" I asked Destiny.

"Call me and often." Destiny answered. "How is Imani doing?"

Destiny was laughing now.

"She's fine. Why?" I asked.

Destiny was still laughing.

"Girl, you know I couldn't help myself. I saw her move away from you during the bouquet toss. I just had to do it." Destiny said. "You should have seen the look on her face. It was priceless."

"She called me on New Year's saying it didn't count because you threw it at her. You are too wrong." I told Destiny.

Destiny laughed so hard she started snorting. I have never heard her do that before. I started laughing also.

"Oh yeah it counts." She finally calmed down but continued laughing. "I'm going to miss you two so much. Meet me for lunch so we can catch up. The moving people here to pack up my apartment then Stephon's so no one will miss me for a while."

I agreed to meet Destiny for lunch at one before we hung up. I don't know why I talk to her at work. She always has me cracking up and then it takes forever to get back into work mode. I'm going to be a mess after lunch. I know she is going to have some funny stories to tell.

At lunch I met a different Destiny. She was a lot calmer and only managed a small smile when I greeted her.

"What's wrong?" I asked her when we sat down at the table.

"Do you think I made a mistake getting married?" Destiny asked.

She didn't even hesitate. It must be serious.

"No! Why would you ask that?" I asked.

"I know I shouldn't have but I spoke to Helena this morning. She called my house after I hung up with you. I checked my caller ID and she had called several times while I was on my honeymoon." Destiny said. "Why is she still calling me?"

Destiny looked sad. I could tell that Helena calling her really bothered her but I didn't know why.

"Why did you talk to her? That is part of the reason that she is calling you. She knows that she can get to you. You love Stephon, right?" I asked hoping she would say yes.

"Yeah you know I do. I am very much in love with my husband. Helena said that I shouldn't have married him until I resolved my feelings for her and for women in general." Destiny said.

Destiny looked around the restaurant, making sure nobody heard her but me.

"Do you still have feelings for Helena?" I asked hoping she would say no.

"I feel I should have never messed with her." Destiny laughed. "Naw, she put me through a lot and I definitely am through dealing with her."

Destiny's answer was not exactly what I wanted to hear but I'll take it.

"What about your feelings for women?" I asked.

I was treading lightly because I really didn't want to hear about that.
"I don't know. Helena is the first woman that I have met in a long time that I had feelings for. I'm not attracted to most women." Destiny kept it simple, sensing my discomfort.

"You said in a long time? There have been others?" I had to ask.

"Yes, but I never acted on it before." Destiny answered.

She didn't offer any more information so I didn't push.

"So what's up with you? How is Darrell?" Destiny was changing the subject and we both knew it.

"We're fine. He's fine." I answered.

We are not fine. Well I'm not anyway. We haven't had sex since New Year's Eve. He gets close and then he backs off. I hesitantly began to tell Destiny what happened on New Year's and what's going on now.

"Damn girl! You mean he just stood there like a mannequin and then squirted?" Destiny laughed then she asked. "What happened to him?"

"I don't know. I didn't think it's that serious but he is still acting like it is the end of the world." I answered.

Destiny started laughing harder. "Damn you sound frustrated. I don't know what to tell you. That has never happened to me before."

Destiny was laughing hard at her own joke. She stopped when she realized I wasn't laughing with her.

"I'm sorry girl. I really don't know what to tell you. Have you tried seducing him? Tricking him into getting it up?" Destiny asked.

"Damn I never thought about that. Thanks." I answered.

"Now we can change the subject. Have you seen the house yet?"

"Not in person but I saw it online. I can show it to you later." Destiny told me.

"Um, not tonight but possibly tomorrow night. Tonight, I have to trick a man into sleeping with me." I said shaking my head.

I was thinking that it is really a damn shame that I have to trick him to get some. Then I thought of how much of a shame it will be if it doesn't work.

Destiny and I ate lunch in utter silence. We both have a lot on our minds. Every now and then Destiny looked up and smiled at me to let me know she is still with me. I did the same. I'm really going to miss her.

"We should go out." Destiny broke the silence. "Yeah call Imani and tell her."

"Are you serious?" I asked. "Stephon is going to let you out of his sight?"

"Yeah! Let's go out one last time. All three of us. Like we used to. He has nothing to worry about. I'm married to him. He'll let me." Destiny answered shaking her head up and down.

"Look at you. He'll let you. Damn you are really married." I joked with her.

"You better be sure that Darrell is going to let you go." She returned the joke. "And we ain't going to his club so he can watch you."

Destiny got the last laugh on that one. Damn how is this going to work? I haven't been out since we got serious.

"Stop trying to think of excuses. Just do it. We're going. Friday! Male Encounters! Saugus. Be there." Destiny said with an evil laugh.

Destiny knew she is starting trouble.

"Alright. Be sure because once I call Imani it's on." I said trying to save face.

"Friday! Yea!" Destiny is so sure.

I'm not as sure because of the way things are going. I don't want Darrell to think I think I want to go somewhere else to get it.

I got back to work, called Imani.

"What are you doing Friday night?" I asked.

I did her like she does me. I didn't even say hello.

She wasn't fazed by it though.

"Why what's going on? Where's the party at?" Imani squealed. "Wait a minute. Where's Darrell?"

"What? What do you mean where's Darrell?" I asked.

Not her too, I thought. "Does everyone think I am on lockdown?"

"I ain't seen you since New Year's Eve. Yes. Heifer! I think you are on lockdown." Imani answered.

"You could have at least hesitated." I told Imani.

I began to tell her that Destiny wants to go out with us one last time on Friday. She picked the Male Encounter show on Friday. Imani began laughing loudly but remembered she is at work and shhh'd herself.

"You know Darrell ain't letting you go to that heifer. You might as well cancel now." Imani started laughing again.

"What? He'll let me go. Why am I saying let? Cut it out." I told Imani. "Go buy something shocking to wear. We're going."

I told Imani bye, that I had to get back to work. I am really going to call Darrell, make sure my mouth didn't write a check that my ass can't cash. I can't believe I am about to ask permission to go out with my friends. I have never been here before but here I go.

I called Darrell at the club.

"Hey. I'm surprised to hear from you. What's wrong?" He asked.

"Nothing is wrong. Do we have anything planned for Friday?" I asked.

I let the dance begin.

"No. I'll probably be here. Do you want to come here?" He asked.

"Actually Destiny wanted to go out for one last time, we planned a girl's night out." I told him.

"OK. You want to have it here?" He asked.

"No. Destiny wants to go to Saugus." I said hesitantly. I was waiting for him to say something.

"OK. Male Encounters huh? She wants to go out with a bang?" Darrell asked.

He started laughing, making me nervous.

"So is this OK with you?" I asked him.

"Hell naw! It's not alright. You want me to let you go watch some other men strip? What I look like a punk? Is that what you want me to say?" Darrell said, still laughing at me.

"That's not funny. I asked you because I didn't know how you would feel about it and you ridicule me. For that, I'm grabbing an ass." I said laughing back at him. "No ser. What time are you getting home tonight?"

"I'm sorry. Thank you for asking me but you don't need my permission to go out." Darrell answered. "I will be home by ten. See you then?"

"OK. Love you." I said.

"Game! All game I tell you." Darrell answered, stealing my words from New Years.

We both laughed at that and then I hung up. I was at my desk feeling good and a little full of myself. Yeah! I don't have to ask him to go out. I began wondering if that is how he really felt or if he just didn't want to say anything. I'll ask him again before Friday.

I knew going to lunch with Destiny was a bad idea. It is almost 4 o'clock; I have gotten almost nothing done. I began to think about the things Helena said to her. Helena may actually be right. It's too late now. Destiny is already married; she says she is happy. Who am I to argue with her? Destiny shouldn't have talked to Helena. Of course she was going to try and confuse Destiny. She wants her.

I got home and cleaned the house, lit incense, and candles then turned-on soft music. I got in a tub of jasmine scented oil after I ordered dinner, laid the very little lingerie that I bought at Victoria's Secret on the bed. I still couldn't believe I was going through all of this to get some. I laughed because men do it all the time. They usually make all the efforts. I am also doing it for him, us.

After I got of the tub, I called Darrell and asked if he could pick up the dinner I ordered. This is to make sure that he is coming home when he said he is. I know he'll make an extra effort if he knows I haven't eaten. He told me that he's wrapping a couple of things up and he would be here soon with my delivery. I hoped so.

When I heard Darrell's truck in the driveway I threw my robe in the hall closet and stood in the entranceway. He came in the door, saw me, and dropped the bag of food.

"You look amazing! Damn!! I said you could go with your friends." Darrell said, laughing it off.

He didn't move any closer to me though. So I went to him. I didn't say anything, just looked at him.

"Baby I'm a little tired. I just want to take a shower and sleep." Darrell said.

"I ran you a bath. Will that do?" I asked.

"Yes. What did I do to deserve this?" He asked.

"You have been really, really good." I said and dropped the lingerie.

Darrell bit his lip then all of a sudden, picked me up and took me upstairs. We didn't even make it to the bedroom. He put me up on the rail above the stairs while he undressed and kissed me all over my face and neck. I prayed this is it. Oh yeah this is it and it feels so good. I didn't know whether to hold the railing or him. Oh damn, I'm going to plunge to my death but what a way to go out.

He picked me up and carried me to the bedroom. He was bouncing me up and down on it while he walked. He went past the bedroom into the bathroom.

"I told you I want to take a bath." He finally spoke as he laid me in the tub.

He took the rest of his clothes off, continued the ride in the tub. I was speechless, well not speechless. The words I said just didn't make much sense. I screamed. Nothing in particular. Just a scream. It was a scream of relief more than anything else.

Darrell laughed and said, "Damn, someone was stressed. I'm sorry."

He dried us off with a towel when we were done. He began laughing again when he saw my hair is a wet matted mess. I didn't care that I am going to be sporting an afro tomorrow, I am happy and satisfied. He brought me out to the bedroom, brought the blow dryer. He dried my hair; put it back in a ponytail before he made love to me again.

I woke up in the middle of the night and found Darrell sitting up in bed.

"What's the matter?" I asked him.

He looked down at me and said "Not a thing. Everything is perfect. I love you so much."

"I hope so; after the way you took advantage of me tonight." I said, trying to make him laugh.

"Oh. I took advantage of you? Oh yeah, I cleaned the food I dropped up." Darrell said, laughing.

"I'm sorry for putting you through that." He continued.

He got serious again.

"I'm fine. You're fine. We're fine. That's all I wanted, for you to be fine again." I told him smiling.

I was still giddy; I couldn't hide it.

"You are amazing. Will you marry me?" Darrell asked.

I looked up at him but didn't answer.

"OK. You don't have to answer right now." Darrell said. "Get some sleep and we'll talk about it this weekend."

I looked at him a little longer then I went back to sleep. I wonder if I'll think this is all a dream in the morning.

CHAPTER 29

I called Destiny from work the next day.

"It's on! Chica. I'm all good for Friday. Darrell said I don't need his permission to go out." I said.

I was still in a good mood.

"I take it my plan worked because you are hyped up." Destiny answered, laughing at my intensity.

"Oh, hell yeah! Damn, I need to do that more often. It felt good to initiate sex." I said. "It felt even better to receive it."

Destiny was still laughing at me. I didn't care how I sounded because it was good.

"He asked me to marry him?" I sprung it on Destiny, almost hoping she didn't hear me.

"What? When? What did you say?" Destiny asked.

"When I woke up after we had sex. That's not a real proposal." I answered.

"What? Why? Denise you are not making any sense." Destiny was screeching now. "I can't believe you. You better not have said no."

"I didn't say anything. He told me I didn't have to answer yet." I told her.

"I can't believe you. Do you want to marry him?" Destiny was still screeching.

"I don't know. I love him but it's too soon." I answered.

"What? Stephon and I only knew each other a couple of months. If it's right you'll know." Destiny answered me.

She sounded totally frustrated with me. I am a little frustrated with me also.

"Do you know Denise?" Destiny asked.

"I don't know." I told Destiny. "I want to get to know him better, for us to progress to marriage."

"You going to mess around and screw this up." Destiny said. "I'm sorry. I didn't mean to say that. I know everyone is different and I also know that if he loves you and you love him and it is meant to be, it will happen. I love you girl and I want you to be happy."

"I understand. I don't want to screw it up. By the way I haven't told Imani and I don't think I am until there is something official to tell. Please don't say anything?" I asked Destiny.

"No problem. I have to go. One of the moving men is trying to get my attention. Take care and think about what you want." Destiny said before she hung up the phone.

I continued nodding at the things Destiny said after she hung up the phone. She is right. I will probably screw this up. I don't know what to say to Darrell but I need to figure it out. I do love him. I don't know what I am afraid of.

We were all at my house on Friday. Darrell decided that he would cook for us before we went out for ladies night. He invited Stephon to the club later but Stephon declined. He told Darrell that he had a lot of cleaning up to do before Sunday.

At dinner the mood was somber. We were all thinking about how much we are going to miss each other but no one wanted to start crying. I know I didn't. Darrell made a toast to the three musketeers. He looked over at me, winked his eye. We all clanked glasses and went back to eating.

When we finished dinner I went to Darrell, kissed him, and thanked him for cooking dinner. Destiny and Imani mockingly did the same before we went upstairs to get dressed to go out. Darrell and Stephon began joking with us.

"Don't worry about all the dishes and stuff. We people with no plans tonight will clean up." Stephon said.

He and Darrell started laughing and then Darrell joined in.

"Yeah I guess we'll just sit around and do nothing. You know men stuff. Honey, do you know where the remote control is?" Darrell added.

We just giggled at them as we ran upstairs. Destiny asked Imani what she had in the shopping bag and Imani said her outfit for the night. Destiny told Imani that the shopping bag was very small and light to have a whole outfit in it. Imani just laughed and mushed Destiny in the back of the head.

Darrell and Stephon were washing the dishes when Stephon couldn't bare it anymore. He had to ask Darrell how he was doing.

"Hey man. How's it going?" Stephon asked.

"Fine man. How's newlywed life treating you?" Darrell asked in return.

"Good. Good. Real good." Stephon answered and looked at Darrell again before he continued. "So everything is good with you and Denise?"

"Yeah. Why? What have you heard?" Darrell asked.

He figured that these questions were a little out of left field for Stephon to be asking because they are not that close.

"I heard you had a rough time of it for a while and I am just wondering if things are better." Stephon answered.

"Rough time? When? Things are great. At least I think they are." Darrell answered.

Darrell was getting annoyed because he had no idea what Stephon was talking about.

Stephon continued, "I heard Destiny talking to Denise on the phone. One of the moving men said he was trying to get Destiny's attention but she was huddled in the corner with the phone. I went up to get her and I heard them talking about your problem. She saw me and quickly hung up the phone."

Stephon stopped, looked at Darrell. Darrell urged Stephon to continue because he still wasn't realizing what Stephon is talking about.

"I asked Destiny about it and asked her if she didn't think Denise should come to you if you were having problems. Destiny told me what happened on New Year's Day and it is nothing you talk about, it's something you fix. She informed me talking about it would only make the situation worse. She said her plan worked so I guess everything is all good now?" Stephon looked at Darrell, shaking his head up and down.

Darrell couldn't believe that Denise told Destiny about what happened.

"Why would she do that?" Darrell asked Stephon. "Why would she discuss our private business with her friends?"

Stephon answered, "Those two aren't friends, man, they are sisters. She did it because she cares about you and wanted suggestions on how she could help you."

"I bet Imani knows too. She doesn't like me anyway; she probably got a real kick out of hearing that." Darrell said. "I don't like this at all man. That was between us."

Darrell was mad and really didn't know what to do. He began thinking he made a mistake when he asked me to marry him.

"I don't want them all in our business." Darrell was fuming. "And no disrespect to you. I don't know you like that; don't want you in our business."

"Damn you better get used to it. These women talk to each other about everything. I'm sure you know plenty of my business." Stephon was a little irritated at Darrell's tone and what he said.

"What business? I know you are married to my wife's best friend and you are leaving Sunday. That's it." Darrell was still angry.

"So Denise never told you Destiny is bi-sexual?" Stephon asked.

"What? No. Hell no. What? Are you fucking with me? You married a bi-sexual chick? Sorry. That never goes well. You should have made her pick a side." Darrell was angry and confused now. "Naw Denise didn't tell me. So not only is my business up for discussion but it's OK to keep shit like that from me."

Darrell started shaking his head. What he really wanted to do is come upstairs and ask me about it.

"Damn, you didn't know? She was outed in your club? You don't know what's going on in any part of your life?" Stephon really didn't mean to say it but Darrell was irritating him.

"I don't know what's going on. From what I heard; your wife got smacked up by her bitch in the middle of the club right in front of you? You have the nerve to tell me I don't know what's going on? I saw the incident report but I didn't know it was Destiny. Damn I heard the bitch was at your wedding too." Darrell laughed madly.

He was still mad at me but he thought this Stephon dude is a punk.

Stephon was staring at Darrell like he had four heads. He

didn't know Helena was at their wedding and he wasn't going to let it slide.

Stephon yelled. "Destiny! Destiny! Come here for a minute darling."

Destiny asked Stephon if it could wait, Stephon told her no.

Darrell started thinking he took it too far in his anger. Oh well, the brother started it, he thought.

Destiny showed up downstairs in a robe and her hair in curlers.

"What baby? I was about to get in the shower." Destiny asked smiling at Stephon.

"Was that bitch at our wedding?" Stephon yelled.

Imani and I heard him from upstairs and came running down.

Darrell began laughing when Imani and I appeared. "You in trouble now man."

Stephon was not amused. He shot Darrell a look, turned back around to Destiny.

"Was that bitch at our wedding?" Stephon asked again.

"Yes she came to the church. Did she have an invitation, stay for the ceremony, and have chicken or beef. No! Who told you that?" Destiny responded.

Destiny knew who told him and was staring right at Darrell.

"Darrell. Why did you tell him that?" I asked.

"I didn't know it was off limits because no one told me who she was. No one tells me anything but my business is up for discussion."

I gave Darrell a puzzled look.

"What are you talking about honey?" I asked Darrell.

"Why do I have this man asking me if my dick is OK?" Darrell continued. "I don't know him like that."

I couldn't say anything to that. Imani was standing there with her mouth wide open. She tried but she couldn't hold it in.

"Denise what did you do to his dick?" Imani asked.

"Not now Imani." I shot back at her.

"Don't act like you don't know." Darrell told Imani. "I'm sure you got a good laugh at my expense."

Imani was just standing there, bewildered. She really didn't know Darrell thought as he looked at her face.

"Sorry Imani." Darrell said to Imani.

"No problem. Are you OK?" She asked.

Imani seemed genuinely worried.

"Yeah I'm fine Imani." Darrell answered. "Thanks for asking."

"Well this doesn't really concern me so I am going to go back upstairs. I'll take my shower while you guys are figuring this out." Imani said before she went back upstairs.

Imani began wondering why there was something she didn't know. She began to wonder if Destiny and I thought we couldn't trust her. She thought about it the whole time she showered and became saddened by the thought they would feel that way.

I started worrying about Imani and her exit. It wasn't like her to want to leave drama and gossip. I am, however, more worried about Darrell and what set him off.

"Honey what is the matter?" I asked him calmly.

I was handling him with kid gloves because of the situation.

"Why did you talk to Destiny about what was going on with our sex life?" Darrell asked.

"I did it because I didn't know what else to do. I tried things to get close to you but they weren't working." I answered.

"And so because she is an expert you decided to go to her?" Darrell snapped.

"No. Because she is my best friend and because of the sensitivity of the issue I decided to go to her." I answered him. "Why? Is that wrong?"

"Because it is none of her business. It is none of his business. You should have come to me and discussed it." Darrell yelled.

"I'm sorry. I didn't know how to approach you about this. It was a new situation for me. You seemed so upset when it happened and then you kept pulling away from me so I didn't know where else to turn. It isn't like I just told her to get a good laugh at you or to have people all up in your business." I told him. I looked at him to gauge his anger. He's still fuming.

"I made a mistake. What I asked you the other day forget about it. You're not the woman I thought you were. Damn, having sex is more important than my feelings? Of course it is, look where you are going tonight." Darrell responded.

His words totally shocked me. How could he accuse me of only caring about sex? I was about to cry but then I thought about it.

"Get the hell out of my house!" I yelled before I even calculated it in my brain.

Darrell turned and looked at me, surprised. "Get out huh?" He answered. "Have fun tonight and have a good life."

CHAPTER 30

Darrell walked right past me and left the house. He just nodded his head up and down then walked out. He didn't slam the door or anything. He just left. I felt like I was struck by lightning. I turned to Destiny and asked if she wanted me to do her hair and if she was ready to have some fun tonight.

Destiny looked over at Stephon, who was as shocked as the rest of us at what conspired. He came over and hugged both of us. When he let go he told Destiny he loved her and for her to never doubt that. He told me not to worry. He said he is not going to tell me it is for the best but that Darrell has a lot of anger inside and directed it at the wrong people tonight.

"I would have understood you did it because you care about me." Stephon said.

"I just think his ego is bruised because he still thinks it is such a big deal. He is upset we know, not at Denise. He'll come around." Destiny said. She was still holding me.

"Thanks. Are we still going out?" I asked Destiny but I was really asking Stephon.

Stephon answered. "Don't let me hold you up. Be good ladies. I will see you tomorrow Destiny."

Destiny nodded and blew Stephon a kiss. She couldn't believe how understanding he is being and wondered if he is really OK.

"Denise, go strike up the curling iron and get Imani out of the shower. I'll be right up." Destiny said, staring at her husband.

Destiny went over to him, kissed him hard. She was holding him so tight. She told him that she is the luckiest woman in the world and that she loves him so much. She apologized for not telling him that Helena showed up but she didn't think it was relevant because she didn't cause any problems. She guessed Helena saw the notice in the newspaper or something and wanted to see if they were really going to get married.

Stephon nodded, told Destiny that he trusts her. He kissed her on her forehead, then on the lips and told her to have fun, but not too much fun. They both laughed as he turned and left the house. She kept waving at him as he walked to his car, then she ran upstairs yelling for Imani to get out of the shower.

When Destiny got upstairs she kissed me on my cheek. Imani was lying on the couch I have in the corner of my bedroom. She hasn't said anything to me since I came upstairs.

"How are you doing?" Destiny asked.

"I'm fine." I answered her, went back to putting on my makeup.

"It will all work out for the best. No matter what that is, it'll be OK." Destiny told me as she wrapped her arms around me.

"What will be alright?" Imani asked.

"Darrell and I broke up, Imani." I answered.

"Why? What the hell is going on around here?" Imani asked. "And why did you feel like you couldn't tell me?"

I turned and looked at Imani.

"I'm sorry Imani. I wasn't trying to keep anything from you. I just happened to be talking to Destiny; she noticed something was wrong with me." I answered Imani's question and hoped it was enough.

"OK I won't ask anything else." Imani said.

At that point, I knew my answer was not enough. I told Imani what happened on New Year's and about what happened downstairs. Imani apologized for being so selfish.

"I can't believe he talked to you like that? It's not that serious. It happens all the time to Jaloni. It probably happens to every man at least once in their life. He's overreacting about everything Denise. I'm sorry." Imani said.

She came over and wrapped her arms around me too.

"I was alright until you two began smothering me. Release me." I said and laughed. "Come on, we're going to miss the show and a sex fiend like me can't have that."

They both laughed and let me go. Imani went back over to the couch and began painting her toenails and Destiny went in the shower. She blew me a kiss on her way to the bathroom. I swatted it away; told her I don't want her sympathy kisses. She blew me another, put her fist up in a threatening manner and told she would get me if I swatted it away. We laughed and she closed the door to the bathroom.

Imani looked up after a while to see if I was OK.

"Denise. Are you really OK?" Imani asked. "We can cancel tonight and just stay home."

"We planned to go out and we are going out. I'm fine." I answered Imani.

"OK. I love you and will be here if you need me. You are always there for me so I owe you that much." Imani said.

I had to turn around and look at her. When I did she smiled.

"I'm going to be fine. I love you too." I told her and returned her smile.

Imani took her outfit out of the bag. I was shocked. It is a long, dark pink silk dress which is full coverage. It had a slit up the back but I think that was more for walking purposes. She looked beautiful. It is just right for the club. Destiny came out of the shower, saw Imani's dress, and asked Imani if she felt OK. Imani shook her head up and down. Destiny told her good because she looked amazing and classy. Then Destiny whistled at Imani. Imani gave her the finger. Destiny laughed, saying, "I was just checking. You can't look like that and be answering to "yo mami" or "Let me holla at you for a second.""

When we got to the club Imani hid behind us when she saw one of the bouncers.

"What's wrong? I thought I would be the one hiding from bouncers tonight." I asked Imani.

"Last time I came here he told me about Jaloni being traded. He let me in VIP because he thought he had a shot because I was single." Imani answered.

"No he didn't." Destiny said. "No, he didn't really think he had a chance. You were newly single, not desperate."

We all laughed at that. The same bouncer saw Imani and came up to us. He told us to come with him so we did. He put us at a VIP table, brought us a bottle of champagne. He told us to have a good night, enjoy the show and that anything we wanted is on the house all night.

I looked at Imani, telling her she's going to have to sleep with him because I'm drinking the champagne. Imani looked scared but then began to laugh. She grabbed the bottle and popped the cork.

"Anything for you. Tonight it is all about you." Imani said.

"I am joking. You better not sleep with that." I told her. "I'll pay him back before that happens."

Imani sighed in relief and then told me she was also joking.

"I didn't ask him for this." Imani said laughing.

The show began and it wasn't that good. Then this one

dancer came out. He was a fine chocolate thick brother. He had the crowd in a frenzy. Someone threw him a dozen roses from backstage. He began coming our way and I began teasing Imani, telling her she is in trouble.

He climbed up on our table; begin to take off his clothes. Then he danced down to our level and gave the ~~dozen~~dozens of roses to me. He winked his eye at me and then laid out on the table on his back, grinding. He did this until we gave him most of our dollars. He then went, danced around the room, finding other willing victims.

I wondered what the roses were for. Destiny saw a card in the middle. The card was from Darrell. It said sorry and I told you to have fun so please do, on him. It also said he hopes I will forgive him and that we can talk this weekend.

I didn't know how to feel about this. I alerted Imani to the fact that she definitely didn't have to sleep with the bouncer because Darrell did this.

"So drink up ladies, he can afford it. Champagne all night!" I told Destiny and Imani.

Destiny was cracking up. "You are wrong."

"Pick a dancer you like. We're going to get a private room, have them dance for us." I was serious.

At first they were hesitant. I called the bouncer over to ask him much that would cost just to let them know I am serious. He told me it is $300 each dancer. I told him to hook it up because my girl is leaving Boston in style. I also told him to make sure it went on the tab the gentleman opened for us and he is not to be told.

"I don't know whether or not you work for him but I am sure I can trust you not to say anything. There's something in it for you." I added just to make sure we are on the same page.

The bouncer informed me he does work for Darrell's

security company, he didn't have instructions to report back to him and he didn't want my money. He added my boyfriend is a very generous employer. I laughed at the fact he called Darrell my boyfriend. I'm not sure if he will be by the time I am done tonight.

Imani and Destiny picked out their choices. I chose the one who brought me the roses. The bouncer came back after the original show was done. I asked where I could get more dollars and he informed me we didn't have to tip them because they get the majority of the money from the private room. I told him to bring 3 bottles of champagne; he shook his head and laughed.

"Boss man must have messed up big huh?" The bouncer said. "No need to answer. I don't want to know. Have fun." He walked off and closed the door when he left the room. He continued snickering as he walked off.

The dancers came in the room and started smiling. I told them to chill out and have some champagne. I also told them to come out of the shirts that they had on. One of them said damn when I told them that but they obliged. One of them asked what music we want to hear.

"The sex fiend wants to hear some R. Kelly of course. Ladies R. Kelly good for you?" I asked Destiny and Imani.

They were cracking up and shaking their heads.

Destiny answered first, "R. Kelly is indeed the man and we are all grown in here right?"

Even the dancers had to laugh at that one.

The one playing DJ asked what song or songs.

"Chill and drink your champagne. We'll get to that. Put the club music on for now." I told him.

He did and sat back down.

We laughed with and talked to them for about an hour while we drank champagne. I pressed the button that the bouncer told me is used to get service. I ordered three more bottles of champagne. Destiny and Imani was cracking up in the background. The person who answered the call asked if everything satisfactory. I told her yes.

The bouncer who has been guiding us around all night brought the champagne and brought a single Cosmopolitan for me.

"I didn't order this." I told him.

"I had orders to bring this to you at midnight." He said.

"Damn he sorry Denise." Imani said, laughing.

"OK. That's all." I told the bouncer.

He looked at everyone. He glanced at Imani, commented on how beautiful she looked before he left. We all burst out laughing when he closed the door.

"OK fellas. Play time is over. Let's do this."

I said. "I want to get really acquainted with you guys and nothing leaves this room. Ever."

The DJ dancer asked what song.

"More and More for the first song and then surprise us. Put each of your theme songs in the mix and do your thing." I told them.

I waved the thick one from earlier over to me. He smiled and came over willingly. He put one leg up on the couch I was sitting on and began to grind in my face. I grabbed his leg and started rubbing it. Destiny watched the one she picked out but didn't touch him, not even when he insisted. She waved her wedding ring in his face and he backed off.

Imani like me is thoroughly enjoying this. The dancer is

giving her lap dance; she is feeling on his chest. We looked over; saw Destiny was uncomfortable. At first, we laughed at her and told her it was her idea to come here. After a while, I called her dancer off.

He left the room and Destiny right after him. I started to go after her but she signaled for me to stay. Shortly after Destiny left the room, Petey Pablo's Freek A Leek came on and the dancer who was dancing for me began to dance to it. It is his theme song and the more he danced, the more I realized why. This guy is a freak. Imani and I were looking at him in shock. He took it all off.

Imani said, "Damn your parents must be proud of you. Damn baby!"

I was laughing at Imani's comment. "Maybe not his mother so much but his father is definitely glad he is representing the family name like that."

That was enough for Imani and me. We thanked them for coming. I gave Freek A Leek; yes it is also his stage name, an extra hundred. He tried to resist but I shoved it in his hand. He definitely earned it.

We were still half laughing, half in shock as we left the room. We went to find Destiny. She was at the bar. I walked up behind her, kissed her and she jumped up.

"What's up with you? Are you alright?" I asked.

Imani pointed out the problem. Helena is in the club.

"Did she say something to you? You want to leave?" Imani asked Destiny.

Destiny shook her head no. She turned to face us,

"Y'all are some sick broads. You should be ashamed of yourselves." Destiny said jokingly.

"It only got sicker when you left. You definitely wouldn't have been able to handle what we saw, old married lady." Imani said to Destiny.

I chimed in, "His stage name is Freek A Leek, it is definitely a fit."

We were all laughing.

"More champagne, ladies?" I asked.

"No Denise. Stop it!" Destiny said.

"OK. But you heard him tonight. He deserves it. This is not hurting him. I couldn't do anything to hurt him as much as he hurt me tonight. I could spend all of his money and it still wouldn't hurt him as much." I told them.

"Make sure that you tell him that when you talk to him." Destiny said. "So he'll know not to say anything like that to you again. You never tell any man or anyone how you feel."

        Helena couldn't take it anymore. She came up to us. Imani started to step to her but Destiny told Imani to stop. Imani took Destiny's left hand and lifted it up so the ring was right in Helena's face.

"Oh so that means something now?" Helena asked Destiny.

"It's meant something since the day I put it on. I love my husband very much." Destiny answered Helena. "Even the other day?" Helena asked. "You wanted to come see me. I know you did."

"If I wanted to come see you, I would have. You're wasting your time. Find another girl to harass. I'm leaving the state Sunday." Destiny told Helena and smiled at her.

"That's why there is moving men at your place? I thought you and your husband were just moving in together." Helena told her. "I wish you well but you'll find another woman. It's not me, it's you."

Imani interrupted, "Scram heifer or I'll put my shoe in your ass."

"So pretty, but such a waste because you are a tacky bitch." Helena said to Imani before she walked off.

Imani wanted to go after her but we held her back.

"She's not worth it, Imani. You look so good tonight, just enjoy it." Destiny told her, "She is bitter because she lost. Come on ladies let's go dance before we get out of here."

As soon as we got on the dance floor a group of guys surrounded us. One of them began checking Imani out and then slowly made his move. He watched her the whole time they danced. When she told him she couldn't dance anymore, he offered to buy her a drink. She told him she is all set with the drinks. He nodded and began to walk off.

Imani grabbed him by the hand.
"What's your name?" Imani asked him.

"Rashaad. What's your name beautiful?" He asked Imani.

She told him her name is Imani. He responded that it is a beautiful name for a beautiful woman. He thanked her again for the dance, told her he had to go. She asked why and he told her he has a girlfriend he loves very much and he didn't want to get into trouble.

Imani thanked him for the dance and for being a gentleman. She told him his girlfriend is a very lucky woman. He thanked her, telling her he is the lucky one. He kept turning back, waving as he walked away. When he got over to his friends, they began clowning him. We could hear them laughing.

CHAPTER 31

Imani asked if we were ready to go. We were. It is almost two o'clock anyway. As we walked to the door Freek A Leek ran up and gave me his card. He said it is for my bachelorette party. I looked at him in bewilderment. I heard it's possibly coming up soon.

I smiled,smiled; told him I would definitely keep him in mind.

Imani said, "Bachelorette party? Coming up soon? What is he talking about?" In all of the commotion I had never told Imani Darrell asked me to marry him. I also didn't tell her because I thought it was a moot point earlier this evening.

I told Imani he asked me Wednesday night after we had sex. I didn't take it as a real proposal. She started in on me just like Destiny did.

"Do you love him Denise?" Imani asked.

"After tonight, I'm going to have to think about that." I answered.

"Yes she does." Destiny answered for me. "But the scarety cat didn't say yes Wednesday."

"Do you think that could have contributed to his tantrum tonight?" Imani asked.

I never thought about that. He never mentioned it again until tonight and I never mentioned it to him. Maybe he thinks I don't want to marry him. I asked Imani for her cell phone. Just as I did a limo pulled up. The driver held a sign up that read Three Musketeers.

Imani and Destiny began laughing and pointing. "Damn, Darrell knows how to apologize." Destiny said.

The driver came up and told us a tow truck is coming to get Imani's car. He told her to take the alarm off. Imani's eyes got big at the thought of leaving her Beemer in the lot with no alarm on it. She took the alarm off when she saw the tow truck pull into the parking lot.

When we got into the limo, there was bottled water on ice and a card which said, "I heard you ladies downed a lot of champagne, you'll need this."

As the driver closed the door, he turned a TV on. Darrell was on tape apologizing to all of us. He said he overreacted and he loves me very much. He told Imani and Destiny to talk me into marrying him, please.

Imani and Destiny complied with Darrell's request. When we got back to the city, I realized that the limo wasn't going to my house. I just went with it. We ended up at Darrell's club. The driver came and opened the door to the limo. We got out and a man dressed in a tux came out and opened the door to the club.

When we got into the club we were led to the VIP room. There was fruit and breakfast on the table. The card read, "Also good for excess champagne consumption." We were laughing. The man who opened the door came in with a cell phone. He gave it to Destiny. Destiny laughed a couple of times and gave the phone back.

I gave Destiny a suspicious look.

"What?" She asked.

"Who was on the phone?" I asked her.

"Do I ask you is on the phone when you are on it?" Destiny said laughing.

She nodded her head to alert me that it was Darrell. She looked around to make sure we are the only ones in the room and then told me he asked if it is safe for him to come in.

We were told to sit down and eat. A waitress came in, served us champagne mimosas.

"Like we need any more champagne." Imani said. "I am going to sleep until Monday. I think he is trying to make us sick for spending all that money."

We burst out laughing again.

"Y'all laughing at me?" Darrell asked.

We were laughing so hard we didn't hear him come in.

"I'm sorry for the things I said to you. I already apologized to your husband earlier Destiny. I still don't think he'll be calling me from St. Louis." Darrell said, laughing.

"Baby, I am so sorry. I know I was wrong on so many levels. I told you before; I never want you to be mad at me. I know you had to be tonight. I will make it up to you for the rest of our lives if you'll let me."

Darrell sounded so sincere and he looked so good.

He had a tux on just like the man that let us in the club. That is the first time I saw him in a tux. It is a beautiful sight.

"You don't get off that easy." Imani said.

She wasn't serious but Darrell looked at me like he believed her.

"What else do I have to do?" Darrell asked.

Imani answered, "Take this food away before I get sick."

We all began laughing again. I actually think it is the champagne that is making us so silly. I think Darrell sensed it too.

"I'll let you ladies go when Denise says I am forgiven." Darrell said. "The food stays too. I'll be in my office."

Imani frowned; Darrell laughed.

He left the room and Destiny began picking at the fruit. Imani still looked sick. I told them I would be right back. Imani said hurry. Destiny said take your time and winked.

I went to his office and knocked on the door.

"Who is it?" Darrell asked.

"It's me, Denise. So this hostage situation is how you think you are going to get your way?" I asked.

"I don't know. The light skin one is looking kind of blue. Or is she blue because she drank over a thousand dollars' worth of champagne?" He said laughing.

"We didn't drink all of that. The strippers drunk some and we poured some over their bodies while they danced." I answered him.

He looked up at me in disbelief. I smiled a crooked grin.

"You mean to tell me that you poured Cristal and Dom on naked men. Couldn't you have used a box of wine or something for that?" He was still laughing. "You were mad at me huh? I'm so sorry, baby. Can I have a kiss?"

"Only if you let my friends go." I told him.

"You wouldn't lie to me?" He asked with one eyebrow raised. "Yeah you wouldn't."

"Troy." Darrell called out. The guy who led us into the club came into the office.

Darrell nodded to him and he left.

"It's done. The hostages have been let go." He said.

I think he is really enjoying this.

The phone rang. He picked it up, handed it to me.

"We're in the limo. We're going to your house. Are you coming?" Destiny asked. "Imani didn't make it. Too bad because that dress is so pretty."

I laughed and then hung up the phone. I looked at Darrell and ran for it. I got to the front door but it was locked. Darrell came out of the office with the key.

"Are you looking for this?" Darrell asked.

"You cheated. Imani threw up all over her dress." I told him.

"Damn! I didn't have the surveillance cameras on."

Darrell was cracking up.

I had to laugh too. I know Imani is going to be pissed in the morning.

"Are we good?" Darrell asked.

I looked at him for a while and then said, "Yeah. We're good."

He walked past me and opened the door.

"That's all I wanted to know. Sleep tight, we'll talk." Darrell said as he held the door open for me.

I kissed him on the cheek as I walked past him and blew a kiss at him as I got into the limo.

        Imani had passed out. I just shook my head. She is definitely going to be mad in the morning. I'll put her dress in the laundry when I get home or take it to the cleaners in the morning. Destiny was still awake, staring at me. She wanted to know what Darrell and I talked about.

"What are you looking at?" I asked Destiny.

"Go to hell Denise. What happened?" Destiny asked.

"Nothing. My talking to you is what started all of this." I said to her and laughed.

"No. Premature ejaculation is what started all of this." Destiny shot back at me.

I just looked at her and we laughed. I told her Darrell and I are good. She smiled, grabbed my hand. When she saw there isn't a ring on it, she got disappointed. I told her, "Drink some of that water and get your strength up." She asked, "Why?" I pointed to Imani.

"I'm not touching her, she stinks." Destiny said.

We started laughing again, Imani almost woke up.

"We shouldn't wake her. She'll only puke again." I told Destiny. Destiny agreed, said she would help me get Imani into the house.

We were silent for the rest of the trip to my house. When we got to the house, Destiny and I began to lift Imani out of the limo. The driver offered his services but we told him that we had her. He smiled at us and shook his head before he pulled off.

We pulled Imani up the walkway, praying she didn't wake up. We got her inside the front door and decided that is as far as I wanted her to go in that dress. She really did stink. I told Destiny to run upstairs to get a robe for Imani.

I grabbed Imani from behind and held her up. I pushed her away from me to try to unzip her dress. I couldn't do it. Imani is heavy. Destiny came back downstairs and immediately began laughing.

"You tried to move Imani, didn't you?" Destiny asked me.

"Shh, before you wake her up." I told Destiny.

Destiny put her hand over her mouth and continued to laugh.

Destiny came over and lifted Imani off of me by her hands. I unzipped Imani's dress from the back and wrapped the robe around her. Destiny moved away when the dress hit the floor and Imani landed back on me. Destiny burst out laughing again and apologized. She said that she thought the dress would land on her shoes.

Destiny came back and helped me get Imani to the couch. I was worried about her waking up, throwing up on my couch but we would have never gotten her upstairs. I got a hanger out of the hall closet and hung Imani's dress outside.

"If Imani sees that she is going to kill you." Destiny said, laughing.

"She won't. I'm going to get up early and take it to the cleaners." I couldn't help laughing myself.

"I need some sleep. Are you with me Destiny?"

"Hell, Yeah. I'll be the one in your guest room snoring." Destiny answered. "Good night Denise."

CHAPTER 32

I woke up to the sound of Imani's cell phone. I wondered who would be calling Imani this early in the morning until I looked at the clock. It is two in the afternoon. It didn't seem like it was going to stop ringing and she isn't answering it so I went to look for it. I found in the hall outside my room in her bag.

"Hello?" I answered.

"Hello. Who is this?" Jaloni asked.

"Jaloni. Hi. It's me Denise." I answered quietly.

I didn't want to wake Imani or Destiny.

"Why are you answering Imani's phone? Is she OK?" Jaloni asked.

"She's fine. She's going to have a little headache when she wakes up but she is fine." I answered.

I began laughing just thinking about last night. Then I remembered Imani's dress hanging outside.

"Should I even ask?" Jaloni asked. "I probably don't want to know what you got into."

"Naw you don't." I told him.

"Why do you sound out of breathe?" Jaloni asked me.

"I left Imani's dress hanging up outside. I am supposed to take it to the cleaners but I overslept." I answered.

"I definitely don't want to know." Jaloni said.

He began to laugh at just the implications of last night.

"So how is everything with you?" Jaloni asked. "How is Darrell?"

"I'm good but I don't know how things are with Darrell." I answered.

"What happened?" Jaloni asked. "He seemed so cool."

"It's a long story and the reason for last night's adventure. Well part of the reason. The other part is Destiny's leaving tomorrow." I answered.

I tried to get Jaloni off the trail. It didn't work.

"So he messed up?" Jaloni asked.

"Yeah, then tried to make it up with his wallet." I answered. "So we bought a truck load of champagne at the club and had some fun."

"Champagne is all you need to say. Imani can't drink that stuff to save her life. So did she pass out?" Jaloni asked.

He began laughing so hard he barely finished the sentence.

He continued when he regained composure. "But she never says no to it."

"She passed out after throwing up everything she has eaten the past few weeks. After we left the club, the limo brought us back to Darrell's club and he had fixed a breakfast buffet. It had the intended effect on Imani. It made her sick." I answered Jaloni's question.

Jaloni began laughing again. "This guy is too funny. Is he mad that you bought all that champagne?"

"I don't know. He never said he is." I answered.

"Well good luck to you, whatever you decide. Tell your drunken friend I called and will call back tonight; tell your other drunken friend I said good luck with everything." Jaloni continued laughing. "You take care. Bye."

I said bye and hung up the phone. Imani began rustling

and asked if she heard me say Jaloni's name. My first instinct was to tell her no and that she must have been dreaming about him but I told her the truth. She said oh OK and fell right back asleep. I am glad because it gives me a chance to take her dress to the cleaners.

When I got back from the cleaners, Destiny was in the kitchen making breakfast. At least I thought it was Destiny. When I got in the kitchen, Darrell was standing there in an apron. I thought about it. I didn't remember seeing his truck in the driveway.

"Where is your truck?" I asked Darrell.

"Around the corner. I didn't know how you would react to seeing it here. I knew you were out because your car was gone." Darrell answered. "How did you sleep baby?" He continued.

"I slept fine." I answered. "Why are you here?"

"Oh. I need a reason to come over and fix my girl breakfast?" Darrell asked.

"If you didn't think you did, you would have parked in front of the house." I answered him bluntly.

"Do you want me to leave?" Darrell asked. "I thought you said we are good?"

"We are good but I need time to sort through this. You not only insulted me, but you also insulted my friends. Then you think because you pull out your wallet everything will be forgiven. It's not that simple." I told him.

He looked disappointed and then his face changed.

"You should have figured that out before you spent all that money on liquor and strippers." Darrell yelled.

"Yes I should have. Do you want me to write you a check for last night? At first, I thought it was a way to teach you a lesson but then I figured out, it's not. Even if I spent all of your money it wouldn't amount to the hurt that you made me feel last night." I answered in a calm voice.

"I don't want your money. I want you." Darrell said. "I said I am sorry so many times last night. I don't know what else to do."

"Give me time. Don't send me stuff; stop by or anything like that. Just give me time to think." I said.

Darrell nodded his head, walked out. This time he slammed the door. Imani rose straight up on the couch and looked around.

"What happened?" Imani asked. "What time is it?

"It's about 3 in the afternoon." I answered.

I didn't mention anything about Darrell being there.

"What was the noise I heard?" Imani asked.

"It was me. I dropped something. Sorry to wake you." I answered.

"Why am I sleeping on the couch? What I'm not good enough to sleep upstairs?" Imani looked around. "At least you put a blanket on me."

She began to smile so I knew she was joking.

"You don't remember anything from last night? You should be glad we didn't leave your heavy ass on the porch." I answered.

"So did you and Darrell make up?" She asked.

I thought to myself, she would remember that.

"Sort of. I asked for time to think things through." I told her and smiled.

"You know Denise, sometimes you have to take the good with the bad. No relationship is going to be all good." Imani said.

I looked at Imani and wondered when she got so deep.

"What heifer? Why are you staring at me like that? I learned that from Jaloni." She said and started laughing. "He loved me and all of my craziness."

"Yes he did." I answered. "I just want Darrell to know that he can't hurt me and think a gift is going to make it all better. It's not about material things."

"Oh, now you want to talk to me? Now that Destiny heifer is gone. I don't want to hear it." Imani answered.

Her response shocked me but I recovered.

"You really were wasted last night. Do you think I got your heavy ass in the house alone? Destiny is upstairs." I told Imani, laughing at her look of shock.

"You have one more time to call me heavy. Why did Destiny get to sleep upstairs? Where's my dress?" Imani asked.

That is one question I hoped Imani didn't ask me.

"The dress is at the cleaners. You had a little accident in it." I told Imani.

Imani looked at me for a minute then I guess she decided she didn't want the details or she remembered the details. If she remembered she didn't say anything. She thanked me for putting the dress in the cleaners and called Darrell evil. Yeah. I think it came back to her.

Imani then asked me what is cooking in the kitchen. I forgot that Darrell was in there cooking and almost let the food burn. Imani and I went to the kitchen. I called Destiny down from upstairs and told her to come get something to eat before Imani eats everything.

They tasted the food and both looked at me.

"There is no way you cooked this food." Destiny told me.

"Why?" I asked.

They both said, "Because it tastes good and you can't cook."

I told them Darrell cooked it. Imani looked at me like she solved a puzzle but didn't say anything. I told Destiny Darrell wishes her and Stephon well. Destiny looked at me like she had a question to ask but like Imani she stayed quiet. We ate the food in silence until Destiny asked what we are going to do today.

We thought it through and realized we couldn't go shopping because Stephon would kill Destiny if she bought anymore stuff. We really didn't have anything planned. Destiny told us she will not be bored on her last day in Boston. I told her I had the stripper's card and could call him over.

"No thanks. I'm starting to think Darrell is right. You are a sex fiend." Destiny said.

She hesitated to see if I was going to laugh. I did.

"You didn't see this guy." Imani said sticking up for me.

"Yeah." I said. "I was joking anyway. I wouldn't want you up in here with your eyes covered.

"What honey? Did you forget your keys?" Stephon answered the door.

He was shocked to see Helena walking away from the door when he opened it.

"What the hell are you doing here? Leave my wife alone." Stephon said in an annoyed tone.

"I came to apologize to her for last night." Helena said. "I don't want any trouble."

"Last night. You didn't see her last night. She went out with her friends." Stephon answered. "That is a good try, though. A last-ditch effort to cause problems."

"I saw her last night in Saugus." Helena answered Stephon.

Stephon shook his head.

"Are you following her?" He asked.

"No. It's not that serious. I was there with some of my friends." Helena told him.

She was offended he asked her that but she decided she was going to make peace with Destiny.

"Do you know where she is?" Helena asked.

"Yeah, I'm going to tell you where she is. I'll give her the message. You're sorry. Although I think pathetic would be a better word." Stephon sarcastically said.

He couldn't understand why this girl would not go away.

"Did you ever stop to think that your wife is leading me on?" Helena asked.

It was almost like she read his mind.

"I'm not pathetic. I love her. I don't want to possess her like you do." Helena continued.

"Whatever. Get out of here before I call the police." Stephon said.

"I called her the other day and told her to meet me. She didn't show up because you came home early." Helena told Stephon.

Stephon was in pain. It had to be true because how else would she know he came home early. Even if she was stalking Destiny, she wouldn't have known he was early because he isn't on a schedule. All he could do is shake his head. He didn't want to let on to Helena he knew she was telling the truth.

"Leave us alone. No! I won't tell you where my wife is. No! She doesn't need another apology from you. No! She doesn't want to see you. I don't restrict my wife from going anywhere. If she wanted to come see you, she would have. It was an excuse not to see you. Are you that stupid?" Stephon told Helena.

Stephon knew it was harsh but damn she needed it harsh. Helena looked at Stephon and began charging toward him. He saw her coming and ran in the house because he didn't want to have to put his hands on a woman. Not even this one. Helena banged at the door for about ten minutes and then went back to her car. She didn't leave. She lowered her seat in a reclining position and laid back.

Stephon called Destiny.

"Your bitch is outside the house." Stephon told Destiny.

"Excuse me?" Destiny answered Stephon's declaration.

"You heard me. She is outside. She tried to attack me and told me you were supposed to go see her the other day. I'm sorry I came home early and ruined that for you." Stephon was more frustrated than angry.

"You didn't ruin anything. I told her that because she kept begging me to come see her. I hung up on her but she called back." Destiny answered. "Why are you taking that tone with me? I'm sorry she tried to attack you."

"Destiny, I have errands to run. She is sitting in her car reclined back, thinking I can't see her. She is crazy and my car is across the street. How am I supposed to get past her?" Stephon was pleading with Destiny.

"Call the police. I don't care what happens to her." Destiny said. "Do you want me to do it?"

"No, I can handle it. I just didn't want you to get mad at me later." Stephon told Destiny.

"Are you OK honey? Do you want me to come home?" Destiny asked Stephon.

"No. You're what she wants. I'll handle it." Stephon said.

He felt better about the fact that Destiny said she used him as an excuse to get rid of Helena. He wasn't sure about it but it sounded better to him.

"Baby, are you listening to me?" Destiny asked Stephon. "I said I'm sorry for all of this and I love you. Call me and let me know what the police say."

"OK. I love you too." Stephon said before they hung up.

Stephon thought he should just go out there and kick Helena's ass if she approached him. He knew he couldn't afford to do it and if Helena has really been talking to Destiny she knew he couldn't either. He thought about what Darrell said to him last night. He shook his head and said out loud. "This is going to work out well." Then he called the police on Helena.

CHAPTER 33

Destiny got off the phone, said she had to go home. She asked if we are alright with it. We asked her if Stephon is OK. She said he is.

"What's the rush then?" Imani asked. "Are you sure everything is cool?"

"No it's not. Helena is parked in front of the house and she tried to attack Stephon." Destiny told us.

Destiny continued rushing around, gathering her things.

"So why are you going there? That can only make things   worse." I told Destiny.

"Stephon is calling the police and I want to talk to them. Let them know I had nothing to do with her coming there." Destiny said quickly.

She kept running around looking for her keys.

"I'm going too. I hope Helena gets what she deserves, to be locked up. I have my keys. Let's go." Imani told Destiny. "We'll find your stuff later."

At that time, I realized I have to go too. If I leave this to them it's bound to get out of hand, especially if Imani instigates the situation.

I told both of them to slow down. I looked at Imani and reminded her she is in a bathrobe. She giggled and then asked me if she could borrow some sweats or something.

Destiny decided she was going to put on more than the shorts she was sleeping in. I reminded them the police were probably not going to respond quickly to a man calling, telling them that a woman has him trapped in his home.

"Yeah Destiny your man is a punk. He should go out there, put the pimp hand down on Helena." Imani laughed at the thought of it.

"Stephon doesn't hit women and I love that about him." Destiny answered Imani.

"That ain't a woman. She wants to act like a man, let her get smacked down like a man. I don't care how she pees." Imani answered, laughing, Destiny still wasn't.

We all got dressed and into Imani's truck. We found Destiny's keys but remembered she didn't have her car. Her car is halfway to St. Louis on a car lift. We had to laugh at her. Destiny finally broke a smile.

At the house, the police were arresting Helena. As soon as she saw Destiny she tried to break their grasp and come to her.

"Do you see what your punk ass husband is doing?" Helena asked Destiny.

"Yes. I told him to do it. How dare you try to put your hands on my husband." Destiny answered her.

"Destiny, tell them this is a mistake. I came over here to apologize to you for last night and he came at me first." Helena told Destiny.

Destiny looked back at Stephon. She wondered if Helen is telling the truth. Stephon must have realized what Destiny was thinking.

"Damn Destiny! You're not buying that shit. You know damn well I didn't go after her!" Stephon yelled at Destiny. "Tell them to take her ass away!"

"Do you need any information from me?" Destiny asked the officer.

Helena shook her head in disbelief.

"He's still controlling you. I bet he beats you too. Do you keep that quiet too? Quiet like us? That's how you like it, secret?" Helena yelled at Destiny.

"You can take her away now. I'll come to the station if there is anything you need from me. Also, can you have her car towed so she won't have a reason to come back here? Thanks." Destiny said calmly.

The officer told Destiny that she can take out a restraining order against Helena but she declined. She informed the officer she would be gone by the time the order tool effect. Destiny then looked at Stephon and asked if he wanted to press charges against Helena. She informed Stephon if he didn't they would have no reason to keep her.

Stephon thought about it, decided he just wanted her gone. He didn't want to press charges but he would take out a restraining order. The cops gave him a card and told him they could file an emergency restraining order for him and his residence. They let Helena go and she stared at Destiny for a long time before she got in her car.

Helena wouldn't leave well enough alone.

She yelled to Stephon. "If it's not me, it'll be another woman. The next one you may never find out about."

She looked at Destiny one last time and then sped off.

"You should have had her locked up." Imani yelled as Helena drove off.

"Naw, she is desperate and pathetic." Stephon responded to Imani. "She'll suffer enough."

"Damn you got here quick." Stephon looked at Destiny. "Were you coming to save me?"

"Yep." Destiny told him.

"What did I interrupt?" Stephon asked.

"Nothing. We finished with breakfast and were trying to figure out what to do with the rest of the day." Destiny answered.

Destiny apologized to Stephon for putting him through the whole Helena thing. She reached up and kissed him on the mouth. She then turned to us and said, "I hope you guys aren't too disappointed but I am going to stay here with Stephon."

I covered Imani's mouth and told her that it is fine. I told Destiny to call us before they leave in the morning. Stephon asked Destiny if she is sure. He told her that he would be OK if she wanted to hang with us. She nodded and said she is sure.

Destiny told us that she loves us and that she is going to miss us so much. Imani backed away from Destiny and shook her head.

"I'm not saying bye to you." Imani told Destiny.

I am actually shocked Imani is taking it so hard. Imani kept backing up and then got in her truck.

I said goodbye to Destiny and Stephon. I gave them a hug; told Stephon he better take good care of my sister. He nodded his head. He looked up at Imani's truck, pointed to tell Destiny to go say bye.

Destiny went up to the truck but Imani wouldn't open the door or the window. Destiny blew her a kiss and walked back toward the house. When I got in the truck I didn't say anything to Imani. I just looked at her.

"Everyone is leaving me." Imani said. "You're going to leave me too one day."

"What makes you think that?" I asked.

"Darrell doesn't live here. He lives in Atlanta." Imani answered. "I couldn't say goodbye to her. Just like I can't let go of Jaloni even though I know I have to."

"Why do you have to let go of Jaloni?" I asked Imani.

"We have separate lives in different cities." Imani answered.

"I don't think he would agree. He loves you and hasn't let go either." I told Imani. "And no matter where I am. I will always be your friend and be there for you."

Imani looked at Destiny's house one last time. For a minute I thought she was going to get out of the truck but she didn't. She started the truck and drove off.

I thought about what Imani said about everyone leaving. It is kind of true. At some time we were all going to have to leave each other. I also thought about Destiny and how much I am going to miss her. I can't believe she is leaving us. No, she is not leaving us. We have been together forever and we will always be together.

DEFINITELY NOT THE END

ABOUT THE AUTHOR

Yvette Way is originally from Boston, MA but resides in Atlanta, GA. She graduated from Curry College in Milton, MA with a BA in Communication and also holds an AA in English. She has been writing since she was a child and has always had a love of books. This is her first novel re-released and she also released another novel this year, Story Of Two.

www.ingramcontent.com/pod-product-compliance
Lightning Source LLC
Chambersburg PA
CBHW052033020726

47501CB00004B/1388